BLOSSOMING LOVE

HILDA STAHL

Other books available
in this Prairie Series:

THE STRANGER'S WIFE

THE MAKESHIFT HUSBAND

Copyright © 1991
Bethel Publishing Company
All Rights Reserved

Published by
Bethel Publishing Company
1819 South Main Street
Elkhart, Indiana 46516

Cover Illustration by Ed French
Edited by Grace Pettifor

Printed in the United States of America

ISBN 0-934998-42-6

DEDICATED WITH LOVE
to my sister in Nebraska
Judith Maureen Raabe

CHAPTER 1

With a tired sigh Laurel Bennett tucked a strand of glossy brown hair back in the thick knot at the nape of her slender neck, then once again bent over the record book on her small oak desk. It was hard to fail a student but she had no choice. Bella Garfield hadn't attended regularly enough to pass fourth grade. It wouldn't be fair to pass her on to fifth only to fail her next year.

A fly buzzed against the closed window and Laurel glanced up with a frown. Beads of perspiration dotted her wide forehead and she wanted to open the window, but she knew the hot Nebraska wind would whip fine grains of sand inside. She dabbed her forehead with her damp handkerchief, then poked it back in the cuff of her sleeve. Perspiration dampened her blue and yellow calico dress and she longed to take a sponge bath and change into a fresh dress.

Something bumped against the west side of the one-room schoolhouse and she narrowed her dark eyes. "Did a student return to play a prank?" she muttered. She shook her head. All the children were expected to rush right home after school to help with chores. The spring of the year was a very busy time for all the homesteaders.

She heard the bump again and impatiently pushed back the straight-backed chair, lifted her cumbersome skirts, and strode across the rough plank floor to the window. None of the students would dare touch her cactus garden, not after the tongue lashings she'd given them for even thinking about it!

For two years she'd tried to grow flowers like Ma had grown in New York State, but the hot wind had dried them and the hotter winds had blown them away. One day in June, while walking the prairie, she'd spotted beautiful blossoms and saw that they were cactus in bloom. The hot wind didn't bother cactus. She'd immediately started a cactus garden at the school and it was her pride and joy.

She peered out the window, then gasped as she saw Mrs. Saunders raise a hoe and chop a barrel cactus. Laurel froze then rapped frantically on the window. "Jane! Stop!" she cried, but Jane Saunders swung the hoe and burst open another barrel cactus. It was as if she'd cut through Laurel's very heart.

With a strangled cry of pain Laurel ran to the door, her skirts lifted high and her heart hammering against the hot, tight bodice of her dress. What had possessed Jane Saunders to do such a terrible thing?

Searing hot wind whipped sand against Laurel as she ran to Jane. Laurel lunged for the hoe but Jane leaped back and held it as a weapon. Wind whipped Jane's faded gingham dress around her thin body and flipped the shabby gray bonnet that hung down her back. "What are you doing, Jane?" cried Laurel. Her breast rose and fell and tears pricked her eyes. Jane knew how much she valued her cactus garden.

"Don't try to stop me, Laurel Bennett," shrieked Jane. The wild look in her eyes frightened Laurel.

Laurel locked her hands together in front of her as she looked helplessly from her lovingly collected prickly pear and barrel cactuses to Jane. In the five years she'd known Jane, she had never seen her like this. She was a good wife to Fred and a patient mother to their three daughters.

"What's wrong, Jane? Why are you doing this to me?" Laurel's voice broke and she trembled.

"You think you can do anything you please and get by with it!" Jane's voice rose and she shook the hoe. "You think you're so high and mighty because you're the teacher. But I won't stand by another minute and watch you flirt with my Fred. You can't steal my husband from me!"

Laurel clutched at her dry throat. "Steal your husband? I...I would never do that!" She forced back the burning flush that threatened to turn her face red. A cold knot tightened in her stomach and she wanted to turn and run. Secretly she'd loved Fred for the past year, but had worked hard at keeping it a secret, especially from Fred himself. What had she done to give herself away to Jane?

Jane swung the hoe again with a violence that made Laurel jump back. The hoe split a barrel cactus that would have blossomed in two months, then she turned to glare at Laurel. "I told the school board."

"You what?" The words tore through Laurel's tight throat and came out in a ragged whisper.

Jane shook a long bony finger at Laurel. "I know what's been going on between you and Fred. I know! And I won't keep quiet a minute longer!"

"Nothing's been going on, Jane!" Cold chills and hot flashes washed over Laurel and she could barely stand on her trembling legs. A hawk cried out from the wide blue sky. Jane's bay mare, Lindy, nickered and shook her harness. "You and I are friends. You know that. I've lived in your home almost five years while I taught school here. I've taught your three daughters."

"And quietly and surely stole my husband," said Jane in a cold, hard voice.

"No! I didn't! He loves you!"

"Do you think I haven't noticed how he looks at you? Don't you know how important you are to him? He would rather ride with you across the prairie to find your precious cactus than stay home to be with me."

A tingle of pleasure shot through Laurel, but she quickly forced it away. "You're wrong, Jane."

Jane shoved back her tangled light brown hair with a jerky movement, but the wind whipped it back across her ashen face. Impatiently she tugged it back and held it to the side of her head. She shook the hoe at Laurel. "He told me he wished I had a body like yours instead of a stick-straight one like I do." She leaned against the hoe as if she had lost all her strength. "Do you know how that made me feel? I know he would rather be married to you."

Laurel's pulse leaped and she frowned. "That's not true!"

With narrowed eyes Jane looked down her long, thin nose at Laurel. "I told the school board and now it's up to them. I told them that I won't have you in my home a day longer."

Laurel gasped.

"You have to be out of my place before dark tonight. I expect the school board to force you to move away. If I had my way, you'd never teach school in Nebraska again!"

Fear squeezed Laurel's heart and she stepped forward only to have Jane fall back a few steps. "How can you do that to me? This is my home. I have nowhere else to go!"

"You should have thought of that before you cast your wide brown eyes on my husband and my home," said Jane in a cold voice.

Laurel pressed her trembling hands to her flaming cheeks. "Don't, Jane. Let's talk calmly about this and settle it between us. No one else needs to be involved."

"Oh, wouldn't you like that?" Jane stamped the hoe against the ground and sent up puffs of dust. "You think you could talk me out of this with your smooth talking tongue, but you can't. I know what I know!"

"Jane, I would never take your husband from you. I want a home and a husband of my own."

"You won't have a chance for that around here any longer. Not with your reputation!"

Jane laughed shrilly and Laurel cringed. "I've

seen to that." She jerked on her bonnet and tied it tightly under her chin. "I'm going home to pack all your things. You pick them up before dark or I'll burn them all!" Jane turned on her heels and ran to her waiting buggy. She flung the hoe in behind the seat, lifted her skirts, climbed in, slapped the reins on Lindy's back and drove away in a cloud of dust.

Her hand clamped over her mouth and her eyes bright with unshed tears, Laurel stood alone outside the schoolhouse and stared across the wide valley that led to rolling hills. A small hill hid the town from her view. The Elkhorn River flowed east of town and new homesteads had sprung up in the past three years since Nebraska had become a state. Since she had started teaching, the school had grown from three students to twelve. The building she started teaching in had been made of sod. When the sod building had collapsed last year, they built the frame building here where the children could run and play without bothering the townspeople. She had been so proud of it.

She groaned. What could she do now? How could such a terrible, terrible thing happen to her? Wave after wave of shame washed over her. She covered her burning face and, with a strangled sob, ran into the schoolhouse and slammed the door. Heat closed in around her. Smells of chalk dust and her own sweat filled the air.

She sagged against the door and tears rose inside her and streamed down her cheeks. Hot wind rattled the windows. "Oh, God, what am I going to do now? I desperately need Your help and Your strength. Oh, forgive me! Forgive me for the terrible sin of loving another woman's husband! I am so ashamed! And now to have others hear the awful truth is more than I can bear." She shook with sobs that left her weak. Staggering to the front of the room, Laurel sank to her chair. She covered her face with her damp handkerchief and sobbed harder.

Finally the tears stopped. She rubbed her pounding temples and tried to ease the pain in her head. Nothing could ease the pain in her heart. She hadn't cried this much since Ma and Pa had died six years ago, leaving her stranded and alone in Nebraska territory. Becoming the teacher here in Broken Arrow had saved her life.

She blew her nose and shivered. Somehow she had to convince the board that she wasn't a homewrecker, but a dedicated Christian schoolteacher with the high standards they had insisted on when she first signed her contract five years ago. They needed her here to teach next year. Teachers were hard to find. Either they wanted to live in the east or move on to Oregon. Already they held her signed contract for next year so that they wouldn't lose her.

"They won't make me leave," she whispered. "They won't." She rubbed her eyes and patted her cheeks. Somehow things would work out right. She couldn't lose her reputation just because she secretly loved Fred Saunders. She had never made an untoward remark to him, nor acted unseemly in his presence. Laurel had longed to fall at his feet and declare her undying love to him, but had always conducted herself in a prim and proper manner. His daughters had always accompanied them out on the prairie in their search for cactuses. His family was always around him when she was. How had Jane guessed her terrible secret?

Was it possible that Fred returned that love?

She smiled, then immediately frowned. How could she think such an awful thought? Fred's love belonged to his wife and daughters, not to a lonely schoolteacher sometimes called a spinster.

The door opened and her heart raced. She leaped up expecting to see the school board. Instead, Morgan Clements walked in, dressed in faded blue denims, a blue-gray shirt open at the neck, and boots on his feet. He pulled off his wide-brimmed gray hat and held it in his powerful, sunbrowned hands. Dampness kept his dark hair pressed to his well-shaped head. With narrowed dark eyes, he studied her thoughtfully.

"Mr. Clements," she said with a stiff nod. She'd seen him in church with his wife and three pre-school children. "What can I do for you?"

"There's no one to take care of my three youngsters." The intensity of his look sent a nervous chill along Laurel's spine. "My wife died two weeks ago."

She pressed her hand to the pulse that beat in her throat. "I am so sorry, Mr. Clements!"

He strode forward, his boots loud on the plank floor, and stopped a couple feet from her. "It's planting time. Time for calving. The garden's not in and the wash is piling high. My kids are runnin' wild."

She frowned questioningly. "Oh?"

"I want you to come home with me to take care of things."

She fell back against her desk and stared at him with wide brown eyes. "What can you mean, Mr. Clements? I am the teacher here. I can't just walk out for another job."

He faced her squarely, his hat in his hands, his booted feet apart. "I heard Arly Larkin talking in the hardward store not more than twenty minutes ago. You have no job here."

She clutched her skirt. "No job?" Jane really had convinced the board to dismiss her!

"I know you're without a place to live. I hear your folks are dead and that you're all alone. I'm offering you my place."

She trembled.

"A home of your own and three kids to mother."

She brushed an unsteady hand over her white face and shook her head helplessly.

"No woman wants to be branded scarlet the way this town will brand you."

"This can't be happening. I am innocent!"

He walked to the front desk where her first grader sat and sank down on it. "Care to tell me the truth? I'll listen and that's more than I can say about the men who will be coming here soon."

A gust of wind rattled the windows as Laurel stood straight, her chin high. "Jane Saunders is wrong about me and her husband. I tried to tell her, but she wouldn't listen. I *am* innocent!" But was she really? She dropped her gaze from the steady look in his brown eyes. "I am innocent." she whispered hoarsely.

"We could be the answer for each other, Miss Bennett." He cleared his throat. "You could mother my children and take care of my home. I would give you the protection of my name. No one would dare speak against you when you're married to me."

"Married?" she gasped.

He nodded.

She knew his reputation and she knew what he said was true. "But we don't know each other except by sight."

"We'll take care of that as we live together."

"But what about...love?"

A shudder passed through him and he gripped his hat brim tighter. "I love my wife and there's no room in my heart for another woman."

"Maybe not now, but what about later? What if you find someone and fall in love? You won't be able to marry her if you're already married to me. Neither one of us would tolerate a divorce."

"That time won't come," he said in a low, tight voice.

She moistened her dry lips. "What about me? What if I fall in love?" Or what if Fred Saunders suddenly became available? This was a hard life for women and Jane wasn't strong. Laurel flushed painfully at the terrible thoughts. She pushed back a stray strand of hair. "I can't even consider your suggestion even though it would indeed help both of us. I won't marry without love."

He pushed himself up and looked her squarely in the eyes. "You could marry for a home of your own."

She'd had a chance to do that twice already and had refused, but suddenly the thought appealed to her. She was twenty-six years old, an old maid, and it was time for her to have a home and a family of her own. But she could never marry a man she hardly knew. "Why don't you hire a woman to tend your children?"

He stabbed long fingers through his thick, dark hair. "That's impossible, Miss Bennett, and I think you know it."

She nodded slowly. She knew there was a shortage of women. "I'm sorry. But I must refuse your offer."

A hopeless, helpless look crossed his face, then was gone so quickly she wondered if she'd seen it. "I am sorry too." he said as he clamped his hat on his head. He strode to the door, his boots loud on the plank floor. He turned and looked at her again and a wave of compassion swept over her.

"Wait," she said, taking a step toward him.

"I don't have time to wait. A neighbor boy is staying with my youngsters while I'm in town for supplies. I must get home."

"I could help you for the summer, but I can't marry you."

He pushed back his wide-brimmed gray hat. "Miss Bennett, you can't live under my roof unless you're my wife. You know what people would say and neither one of us wants that."

She flushed. "You're right, of course."

He nodded and again turned to leave. She held her breath as he opened the door. A gust of wind whirled sand inside.

"Wait!" She ran to him and he turned to study her. "Give me some time to think it over."

"There is no time. None for me and none for you."

Sand stung her skin. The team of horses at the hitchrail nickered and rattled their harness. "I am sorry, Mr. Clements. I trust you'll be able to find someone."

"Not likely, Miss Bennett." He gave her one last look, strode to his wagon, leaped easily onto the seat and drove away, the wagon swaying and creaking.

With her hand, she shielded her eyes against the bright sunlight and watched until he was out of sight. For one daring second she wanted to run after him and shout for him to take her with him. Maybe she could catch up with him in town before he left for his homestead.

"What am I thinking?" she asked in horror.

Slowly she walked around the school to stare at her once-beautiful cactus garden. It had been the only thing that had truly been hers, that and the clothing and a few items that she kept after Ma and Pa had died. She'd had to sell the horses and wagon and furniture to keep from starving that first year. She sighed. Jane probably had her trunk packed and waiting.

She heard hoofbeats and ran to the front of the school to see four men riding from town toward her. "The school board," she whispered, trembling.

Arly Larkin led the pack and his face was dark with anger. He slid off his roan before it stopped and walked toward her, his short legs pumping up and down. Wind ruffled his gray hair. He ran a thin finger under his stiff white collar.

"Laurel, we want to talk to you." He motioned toward the men who had dismounted and were coming to stand behind him. "We figured we'd better get this thing settled right away."

Laurel lifted her chin a fraction and forced back the panic rising inside her. "Shall we talk inside out of the hot wind?" She led the way into the schoolhouse before anyone answered. One by one the men trooped inside, all looking very determined. She knew them all very well: Arly Larkin, Grove Mayberry, Bailey Simms, and Jack Cannon. In the past five years she had to answer to them for every action, every penny spent in the school, and what she taught. Nothing had ever been this drastic.

Arly smoothed his hair in place and cleared his throat. "I won't beat around the bush, Laurel. I want to know your side of this situation with Jane Saunders and her happy home."

Anger rushed through Laurel and she clenched her fists at her sides. "You don't want to hear the truth, Arly! You won't believe me when I say that I'm innocent. And I *am* innocent. I would never break up a home." She looked at the closed faces around her. "You men should know me better than that. We've gone to church together these five years. You've watched my every move around town and here at school. Why should you believe Jane instead of me?"

"She's a respectable married woman," said Grove Mayberry in his high-pitched voice that Laurel had never liked.

Murmurs of agreement momentarily drowned out the sound of the constant Nebraska wind. Laurel's heart sank and she ducked her head. "I am innocent." she whispered.

"We're closing school now. If you have the report cards filled out, I'll deliver them in person," said Jack Cannon as he rolled his hat brim with his square red hands. "Them students don't need to know your shame."

"Why won't you listen to me?" Laurel's voice rang out and the men looked at her in surprise. "Can you really send me away when you don't have a teacher for the fall?"

"We'll worry about that," said Arly stiffly.

"But I signed the contract!" She looked from one to another.

"We tore it up," said Bailey Simms with a slight cough. "Tore it up."

Sparks flew from Laurel's eyes. "You can't do that!"

Arly shrugged. "It's already done." He held out his thin hand. "Don't take it so hard, Laurel. You can get another school. You got to understand how it is with us. We can't keep you here with them rumors flying around. Think of poor Jane Saunders."

"What about me?" snapped Laurel. "You're throwing me away just as you do your slop."

"You should've thought of that before you started making eyes at another woman's husband," said Bailey Simms coldly. "We as a school board nor we as a church board will put up with that. You can't expect us to."

"No matter if I'm innocent?"

They stared back at her and then all turned together toward the door. Arly said over his shoulder, "You have to be out of town by nightfall."

"Did you forget the tar and feathers?"

"Don't be bitter, Laurel. We're only doing our job."

She clenched her fists as they slammed the door. She heard them ride away, but she didn't move. She felt like kicking the pot-bellied stove, but knew she'd break a toe and not ease her anger. A cry of outrage rose inside her, but she forced it back. Anger wouldn't change anything.

Finally she walked to her desk. Two report cards still needed to be written out. "Let Arly do it." she snapped. She lifted her drawstring purse from the drawer, opened it and dropped in her pen and ink.

Where could she go?

A tear trickled down her cheek. She had relatives in New York and in Oregon. She shook her head. She had to find another school. She could go to Omaha to talk to Mr. Sooner. He had told her before that he had many schools needing teachers. But what if Arly wrote to him about her conduct? Mr. Sooner would never place her in Nebraska.

So, why not leave Nebraska? Leave the wind and the heat and the blowing sand and the freezing winters? But what of the wide blue sky, the tiny prairie flowers, the crisp winter air?

With a low moan Laurel walked around the room. She picked up books that she'd bought for the school and longed to take them with her. Finally she lifted her bonnet off a hook and tied it in place. God knew her plight and He would help her just as He always had before. Things looked hopeless now but that would change. She'd find someone in town who would drive her to Pine Bluff to the hotel. From there she could ride the train to Omaha.

Suddenly the door burst open and Fred Saunders stepped in and jerked to a stop when he saw her at the coat hooks. "What's this I hear about you leaving Broken Arrow? Leaving the school? Leaving us?" He stood before her, tall and lean with his wide-brimmed hat pushed to the back of his head. Dust covered his work clothes. She knew he had plowed his fields from first light and had probably stopped because someone talked to him about her. She flushed painfully, suddenly unable to look in his dear face. What would he think of her if he knew the depth of her feelings for him?

She cleared her throat. "I don't want to leave, but I must."

He raked his hat off his head and rubbed an unsteady hand over his face and hair. "Jane said she'd do this but I didn't believe her." His blue eyes narrowed into fine slits. Lines fanned from the corners of his eyes and ran into his damp hair.

Laurel clutched her purse tightly.

Fred slapped his hat against his leg, sending dust flying. "Oh, that woman! How could she hurt you? I'll never forgive her for this!"

"Don't talk like that, Fred." Her voice broke and she couldn't go on.

He caught her icy hands in his and held them tightly. She struggled to pull free, then gave up. Her heart lurched as she stared helplessly up at him. His calloused hands felt warm and strong and she never wanted him to set her free.

"Don't leave me, Laurel," he whispered.

Shivers of delight ran down her spine. "Don't, Fred. Please."

"I need you!"

His words wrapped around her heart. She wanted to lean against his broad chest and stay there forever. "You have a wife and family," she whispered.

"God, help me, I know it!" He dropped her hands and stepped back. His face looked haggard and suddenly old.

Scalding tears pricked the backs of her eyes. "I must go," she said softly.

"Not yet!" He reached out for her, then dropped his hands to his sides. "Laurel, do you care at all for me? I must know so that I can survive these next miserable years."

"Oh, Fred!"

"Don't look at me that way, Laurel. Your eyes are wide with a longing that breaks my heart."

Abruptly she turned away. "No, no. This isn't

right."

"I know. But what can we do?"

"We must forget about each other and go on living." A sharp pain stabbed her heart and she moaned.

Gently he turned her to him and lifted her face. Her strength to resist melted away as her eyes locked with his. "I love you, darling Laurel."

"Don't," she whispered.

"Don't shush me. Please. We can go away together. Tonight."

The temptation overwhelmed her and she found herself nodding in agreement. "But it's wrong, Fred."

"I know and I'm in agony over it, but I can't lose you." He lifted her hand to his cheek. "We'll meet here at the schoolhouse just after dark and we'll ride away together and find a place where no one knows us. We'll make a new start. Together." He cupped her face with his hand and her very bones melted so that she couldn't turn away. "I want you desperately. I need you. You know that, don't you?"

"Yes," she whispered, knowing her own need.

He stepped back from her and rammed his hat on his head. "Tonight! I'll be here with the wagon."

She nodded, unable to speak.

A muscle jumped in his jaw and he whirled around and strode away to his waiting horse at the hitchrail. Laurel heard the hoofbeats and ran to the doorway to watch until he rounded the bend to town. Blood roared in her ears and she sagged weakly against the door frame. Could she run away with Fred?

Impatiently she walked out of the schoolhouse and closed the door until tonight. She wouldn't think, she'd do.

Wind blew against her as she walked along the dusty road toward the Saunders homestead. Thankfully she didn't have to go through town and face the ugly stares of the townspeople, nor the pained look on Morgan Clements' face.

She glanced up at the blue sky that stretched on and on until it reached down, down, down to touch the new green grass of the gently rolling hills. Glancing back at the schoolhouse and the two-hole toilet, Laurel thought they looked strange as if someone had plunked them down in the middle of nowhere. It was no longer *her* school. Would it sit empty in the fall or would they find a teacher?

Pressing her lips tightly together, she veered off the road onto the faint tracks that led to the Saunders homestead. She had watched Ruth grow from a year-old toddler to a six-year-old first grader. Priscilla and Marion were third and fourth graders, the top in their classes because she worked with them at home and during the summer. What would the girls do without their pa?

Laurel stopped short with her back to the wind and her head down. Wind pressed her skirts against her legs and the hot sun burned through her bonnet. She looked helplessly up at the wide blue sky. "Lord, what am I doing? The girls desperately need Fred. They couldn't survive this wilderness without him. Oh, what have I been thinking? I can't steal Fred away from his family!" She sobbed and covered her mouth with the back of her hand.

Could she face Fred and tell him that she would not go away with him, that he belonged with his family?

"I can't," she whispered in agony. She shook her head and sniffed hard. If she saw Fred alone, she'd never find the strength to tell him. "I must walk away from here alone."

Could she face life without Fred? But if she went with Fred, could she face herself for what she'd done to his family? She shook her head.

In the distance she saw a cloud of dust and heard the pounding of hooves. "Fred!" Frantically she looked around, then ran away from the trail and behind a grassy knoll. She dare not meet Fred now or she would give in and run away with him.

She knelt behind the knoll and waited, her heart in her mouth, her breast rising and falling. Ants crawled across the toe of her shoe and she brushed them off. She peeked around the knoll and watched him gallop along the trail toward his place. Love for him rose in her and she clamped her hand to her mouth to keep from crying out to him. A cloud of dust billowed out behind him as he headed for the clump of cottonwoods that lined his homestead.

With a cry she ran toward the dust cloud, shouting, "Fred! Come back. I'm here!"

The wind flung her words back in her face. He couldn't hear her. She stood with her hands over her heart, her purse dangling from her wrist. When he was out of sight she slowly walked to the trail and turned toward town. She would send Dale Givers for her trunk so she wouldn't have to face the family. It would be better that way.

She reached the dusty road just as a wagon rolled into sight around a hill. She heard the creak of the wagon and the jangle of the harness. How could she face whoever was in the wagon? She knew the driver had seen her and it would look foolish to run away and hide. With her head down she continued toward town and toward the wagon. Finally she glanced up, then stopped short. It was Morgan Clements. She knew his homestead was in the opposite direction. The strength drained from her body and she waited until he pulled up beside her.

He looked down on her from his perch high above on the wagon seat. She flushed at his steady gaze, but didn't turn away.

"Miss Bennett," he said doffing his hat.

"Mr. Clements," she whispered.

"I stopped at the school but you were gone. I came to make my offer again."

Her pulse leaped. "Oh?"

"I just came from the general store. I know you have to be out of town by nightfall." he gripped the reins tightly. The horses moved restlessly. "Will you change your mind and come with me?" His dark eyes bored into hers and she trembled. "My kids and I need you. And you need us."

She sagged against the wagon wheel. "Mr. Clements, I don't know what to do."

"Yes, you do."

"How can you say that?"

"You have nowhere to go but with me. Unless, of course, you mean to run off with Fred Saunders."

Color stained her cheeks and she dropped her gaze to the toes of her dusty shoes peeking out from under her dusty skirts. "I had planned to do just that."

He sucked in his breath. "And now?"

She lifted grief-stricken eyes to his. "I can't take him from his family. I love him, but I can't...can't break up his home."

Morgan Clements nodded. "I didn't think you could."

"You didn't?"

"No, you're not that kind of woman." He reached his hand down to her. "Get in. We'll pick up your things and be on our way.

She hesitated, then slowly reached up to meet his hand. His calloused hand closed over hers and she stepped up on the wheel and into the wagon. As butterflies fluttered in her stomach, she sat beside him. "I will marry you, Mr. Clements, and I will be a good mother to your children."

He smiled slightly. "Call me Morgan."

"Morgan," she said softly.

"Laurel," he said just above a whisper. He settled his hat firmly in place and turned the team around with a slap of the reins and a click of his tongue.

"What are you doing? What about my trunk?" She looked over her shoulder toward the Saunders place.

"First we'll get married and then we'll pick up your things. It's better that way."

She bit her lower lip and turned to face the road ahead. Was she having a terrible dream? Would she wake up in the room that she shared with the three Saunders girls to find that she had overslept on a school day? Surely her well-ordered life hadn't been disrupted so disastrously!

Morgan glanced at her. "Pastor Elders is expecting us."

Laurel's eyes widened in shock as she stared at Morgan. "He is?"

Morgan shrugged his broad shoulders. "I had to speak with him to make sure he would be around to perform the wedding. If there was going to be one." He cocked his dark brow. "His wife is readying things now."

"Do they know that I'm the woman you plan to...marry?"

"No. I didn't mention that."

The wagon swayed and she braced her feet against the wagon bed and grabbed the seat. "Do they... know the gossip about me?"

He was quiet for a while. "Yes."

She groaned. "Maybe it would be better if I left Broken Arrow altogether."

"Running away is never the answer. The gossip will stop once you're married to me."

"I hope so," she whispered.

She watched a cottontail hop from one clump of grass to another. She saw a large prickly pear and tears sprang to her eyes. Never again would she ride across the prairie with Fred and the girls in search of cactus.

A few minutes later they rounded the bend and Laurel caught sight of the small town. Two horses stood outside the hardware and feed store. A man loaded a wagon outside the general store. Arly Larkin peered out of the doorway of his hardware store and Laurel wanted to sink out of sight, but she lifted her chin and squared her shoulders. Never would she allow the school board to know how close to the truth they'd come about her. Nor would she let them know how upset she was over losing the school.

"Smile at me," said Morgan in a low voice. "Don't let them think that you're heading for the gallows."

She forced a smile that she knew would look real to anyone watching. She knew several people were watching.

"That's better, Laurel." Morgan smiled but the smile didn't erase the pain in his eyes.

A few minutes later he reined up outside the tiny white church. He jumped down and dust puffed up around him. He reached up for her.

Suddenly she couldn't move. What was she doing? Had she lost her senses? She stared down in horror at Morgan Clements.

CHAPTER 2

"I can't go through with it, Mr. Clements," Laurel whispered hoarsely as she looked down in anguish from her high perch on the wagon at Morgan standing on the ground. Hot wind blew dust along the street and past the church. Morgan's team shook their harness. "I can't!" she cried.

Morgan gripped her wrist. "Yes, you can."

She pried at his long fingers, but couldn't pry them loose. "I don't know what I was thinking. This is absurd!"

He nodded. "It seems that way, but it is the best for both of us. I need you and you need me."

"Oh, what have I done?" Tears burned her eyes as she stared at the restless team hitched to Morgan's wagon.

Morgan tugged gently on her wrist. "Come here, Laurel. Please. Please."

Finally she turned to look down at him and the tender, understanding look on his sun-darkened face pushed away the sudden fear. She gave him her other hand and leaned toward him.

He lifted her down and she stood between him and the wagon with her hands in his. Her long calico skirt brushed against his legs and the tops of his dusty boots. She could smell his sweat and the leather of the harnesses.

"Don't be frightened, Laurel," he said softly.

"Are you very sure this is what you want?" she whispered.

He nodded. "I'm sure enough for both of us."

She sighed and ducked her head. She knew her clothes were covered with dust and sweat. Her hair was in tangles under her bonnet. "This is not the way I pictured my wedding day."

"I know." He squeezed her hands. "Just pretend we're dressed in beautiful wedding attire and that all of our friends are here to witness this wonderful time."

She laughed weakly. "I'm afraid my imagination isn't that strong."

Just then a dark cloud passed over the sun. Shivers ran up and down Laurel's spine. A dog barked and children shouted back and forth up the street. A man rode past on a mule with a long rifle in his hand.

"Shall we go inside?" asked Morgan.

"Yes," she said, dusting herself off the best she could.

He walked with her through the front door of the little church with his hand at her waist. She stopped and looked at the straight-backed wooden pews that stood in tidy rows, empty and waiting for the congregation. Vases of lilacs at the small table near the front of the church covered the usual smell of the musty hymnals. Sunlight shone through the windows onto a small organ.

"I'll get Pastor Elders." Morgan's voice sounded loud in the small church and Laurel jumped.

Just then the back door opened and the pastor and his wife walked in. They both were dressed in black. Laurel tensed as they stared at her. Color flooded her face and she stepped closer to Morgan for strength.

"Laurel, what brings you here?" asked Pastor Elders stiffly.

Laurel could only stare at the heavy-set man and his round wife.

"Did you come to be a witness?" asked Mrs. Elders sharply.

"Laurel has agreed to be my wife," said Morgan softly. He slipped a strong arm around her slender waist and pulled her tight to his side. "We're ready to begin when you are."

Mrs. Elders gasped and her heavy bosom rose and fell. Her husband shot her a warning look and she didn't speak, much to Laurel's relief. Mrs. Elders was known for her outspoken manner.

Pastor Elders motioned for them. "Stand here, please."

"Do you want organ music?" asked Mrs. Elders stiffly.

"No," said Morgan as he led Laurel to stand at the altar.

Laurel's heart hammered so loud that the words the pastor spoke over them were almost drowned out. The room whirled then righted itself with a jolt as he pronounced them husband and wife. She gripped Morgan's arm tighter and felt his look, but couldn't lift her eyes to meet his.

What had she done? This had to be a bad dream. She was not an impulsive woman. Would she live to regret her sudden decision?

What was Morgan thinking right now? Was he sorry for his rash action? She peeked at him from under long, dark lashes as he paid Pastor Elders. Laurel bit her lip. Morgan looked sure of himself and not at all sorry. She breathed easier and was able to smile slightly as they said goodbye.

Mrs. Elders caught at Laurel's arm. "Come with me, my dear."

Laurel shook her head. She knew Mrs. Elders wanted to hear every detail that led up to the marriage. "We must get back to Morgan's children before dark. I'll see you when I come to town again."

"I hope you haven't made a hasty decision," said Mrs. Elders.

"It's too late now," said Pastor Elders, circling his wife's plump shoulders with his arm. "Let them be."

Mrs. Elders scowled at her husband, but he smiled and winked and finally she smiled too.

Outdoors Laurel leaned weakly against the wagon bed, her head down as the wind blew against her back. Faintly she heard a dog bark and children shout. She turned to Morgan, only to see a stricken look on his face. A band squeezed her heart. It had been as hard on Morgan as it had on her! She reached out to him with a trembling hand, then dropped it to her side without touching him.

The horses moved restlessly and the sorrel nickered. Morgan settled his hat firmly in place and
caught Laurel's arm. "Ready?"

She nodded.

He lifted her to the high seat, then sprang up
beside her. He unwound the reins from the brake and
slapped them against the horses. "Do you need
anything from town before we go?"

She straightened her skirts and retied her bonnet.
"Not that I can think of right now."

"It'll be a while before we come to town again."
He cocked his brow and she shook her head. He
drove away from the church to turn around on the
far side of it.

Laurel sat with her back stiff and her head high.
A windmill squawked. The wind had died down
and the sun didn't seem as hot. She felt the stares of
the few people on the street. She knew her marriage
would be the talk of the town for a long time. The
school board would hear and wonder and hopefully
regret their rash action. Maybe they'd even beg her
forgiveness and she just might give it if she was in
the right frame of mind.

She swayed with the wagon, her feet braced on
the rough floor and her hands clasped over the purse
in her lap.

Outside of town Morgan said, "Are you prepared
to face Fred and Jane Saunders?"

Laurel shuddered. "No, but it must be done."

"Yes. Yes, it must." His words were almost lost
in the creak of the wagon.

She watched a jack rabbit stand tall, look around and bound away out of sight. A crow cawed and landed in the path of the horses. It flapped its black wings awkwardly and flew away again.

Laurel's thoughts whirled as Morgan drove off the road and down the faint trail that led to the Saunders homestead. She wanted to jump from the wagon and hide as Morgan drove past the cotton-woods and into the yard. Chickens scattered, squawking and flapping their wings. A horse whin-nied from the corral beside the sod barn. Laurel's nerves tightened and she wanted to ask Morgan to drive away without her trunk, but she bit her tongue. He stopped the team in a flurry of dust.

Laurel glanced around just in time to see the front door of the small house open. Jane stepped out with the three girls close beside her. Jane rubbed her hands down the flowered apron that covered her brown everyday dress. The girls started to run for-ward but Jane stopped them with a sharp word. The color drained from her face as she stepped forward. She glanced questioningly from Morgan to Laurel and back again.

Morgan dropped easily to the ground, reached up for Laurel and swung her to his side. "We came for my wife's trunk," he said.

Jane swallowed hard and frowned. "Your wife?"

Laurel wanted to speak but couldn't find any words. Her hands suddenly felt ice cold.

The girls started forward toward Laurel, but once again Jane stopped them with a low command.

They stepped closer to Jane and stared at Laurel and Morgan with wide questioning eyes. Laurel wanted to assure them that everything was all right, that everything was just the same, but she knew it wasn't. She waited for Morgan to speak.

"Laurel Bennett is now my wife," said Morgan with a slight smile. "We came to get her trunk so that we can head home."

Jane gasped and grabbed at her throat. She swayed slightly, but caught herself and stood straight with her head up. "Laurel? Is this true?"

Laurel nodded.

"Where's the trunk?" Morgan stepped forward. Laurel couldn't move from the wagon for fear her legs would give way and she'd fall to the ground.

"I'll show you." Jane turned and walked to the door. "Girls! Come with me." She waited for them to go in ahead of her, then she followed Morgan inside.

Laurel leaned weakly against the wagon, her eyes closed.

"Laurel!"

She jerked up at the sharp whisper and turned to find Fred standing at the corner of the house, his hat in his hands, his face haggard. "Oh, Fred," she whispered with a shiver.

"I can't come to you or they might see me. But I must tell you something." He scraped a trembling hand over his jaw. "I...I can't leave my family. I won't meet you at the school tonight. I'm real sorry."

She clenched and unclenched her hands at her

sides. "Didn't you hear? I am married."

"Married?" He looked shocked, then stricken.

She nodded. "To Morgan Clements. I knew it was wrong to think of going...away with...you."

Fred stared at her in anguish, then spun around and disappeared. She stood rooted to the spot, wondering if she really had seen him and talked to him or if she had imagined it because she desperately wanted to see him one last time, right or wrong.

The door opened again and Morgan strode out, the humpback trunk balanced on his shoulder. She knew it was heavy, but he carried it as easily as she carried kindling to start a fire. She shot a nervous look around to make sure Fred was out of sight. He was and she felt thankful, yet disappointed. What did she want? For him to leap out and snatch her from Morgan and claim her for himself? The terrible thought filled her with guilt and she couldn't look at Jane or the girls as they stood at the door. The girls sobbed and Jane murmured for them to hush.

Morgan swung the trunk into the back beside the supplies he'd picked up in town. He walked to Laurel and said in a low voice, "Tell the girls goodbye. Can't you see how upset they are that you're leaving?"

She had only been thinking of herself and she turned to face Jane and the girls. Somehow she managed to smile. "I've enjoyed sharing a room with you girls and I had fun teaching you. Maybe I'll see you when I'm in town sometime." Oh, why had she said that? She couldn't face them, knowing what she had almost done to them. "Next year you'll have a different teacher. Help her just like you did me. Goodbye."

"Goodbye," they cried. They would have rushed at her for hugs and kisses, but Jane stopped them with a sharp word.

"Goodbye, Jane," Laurel said stiffly.

"Goodbye, Laurel," Jane licked her lower lip with the tip of her tongue. "If I've said anything to you out of the way, was wrong about anything, then I am sorry."

Laurel nodded and turned to Morgan. His grip tightened on her arm as he helped her up onto the high wagon seat. She moved over and he swung up beside her. He clucked to the horses and slapped the reins and the team stepped forward briskly. Chickens squawked and ran out of the way.

The trees blocked out the sunlight for a few minutes and then the wagon rolled into the bright sun on the open prairie.

"You talked to him, didn't you?" asked Morgan gruffly.

She glanced at him in surprise, then looked quickly away. "How did you know?"

"I saw it in your face and the way you stood." He sounded impatient with her and she lifted her chin defiantly.

"You know how I feel about him, so don't make me feel any worse than I already do," she snapped.

"It's hard for me to believe that you would consider going away with the man."

She pleated her skirt with trembling fingers. "I don't want to talk about it."

He slowed the team and turned to study her. She lifted her chin and returned his look. "Am I going to have to worry about you running off with the man if he comes after you?"

Her dark eyes flashed. "Do you even need to ask?"

A muscle jumped in his jaw. "I didn't think so but it seems I do."

Her stomach tightened. "I suppose I deserve that."

He rubbed a hand down his faded blue denims. "No, no, you didn't. I am sorry. I know I can trust you."

His words pleased her and she relaxed slightly. "Thank you. To answer your question, you won't have to worry about me or about Fred. He talked to me at the house just now only to tell me that he could never leave his family to go away with me. So, you see, you have nothing to be concerned about." She didn't know if she was trying to convince him or herself. Never in her life would she have thought of falling in love with a married man, let alone run away with one. Now, here she was married to a stranger because of her indiscretion, because of her sin. The word *sin* burned her heart and she squirmed.

Without answering, Morgan slapped the horses and shouted to them. The wagon swayed as the team trotted off the trail across the prairie toward his homestead. Laurel bumped and bounced until she balanced herself better and hung on tighter. The seat seemed to grow harder as time passed. The prairie stretched on endlessly. A windmill whirred in the wind, pumping water into a big wooden tank for cattle and horses.

She turned to ask Morgan how much farther to his homestead, but the closed look on his face made the question die in her throat. Was he regretting taking her as his wife?

She thought of the last time she saw Rachel Clements. They had been in church with their three children. Rachel was expecting another baby. The look of love that passed between Rachel and Morgan each time their eyes met had made Laurel envious. The children were shy and well-mannered.

Laurel retied her bonnet as she peeked at Morgan again. She felt his tension. How hard it must be on him to remarry so soon after his beloved wife's death! She knew he'd married her for his children's sake. It made her respect for him grow.

"He's a fine man." she whispered.

He pulled on the reins and the horses slowed to a walk. The silence felt good to Laurel's ears. She turned to him and let the admiration she felt for him show in her eyes. He didn't seem to notice.

"This is going to be hard for me, but please be patient with me," he said without looking at her. "My kids need a mother." His voice broke and he looked at her, then quickly away, but not before she saw the moisture in his eyes.

She blinked back sudden tears. "I will do my very best for you and for them. I promise."

He nodded without looking at her. "I know you will." He cleared his throat and moved restlessly, the reins loose between the fingers of his large hands. "I will be a friend and companion to you, Laurel, but I'm not...ready to be...be a husband."

She flushed with embarrassment. She had been too busy thinking of other things to think of their marriage arrangements. "I'm not...not ready to be a real...wife to you, either."

"Then we're agreed," he said.

"Yes," she answered.

He didn't speak again until they rounded a hill and she spotted a small frame house, a frame barn, an outhouse and a sod chicken coop. Three cottonwoods stood to the north of the house and the prairie stretched for miles on every side to meet the darkening wide blue sky.

"Here's my place," he said with great pride in his voice. "Two years ago I built the frame house and let the chickens take over our old sod house." He stopped the horses and turned to face her. "This is your home now, too."

Her home! The thought of it made her giddy, but she managed a small smile. "I'll do my best to make it a happy home," she whispered.

"Thank you." His brown eyes crinkled at the corners as he smiled at her. His tension was gone and she was thankful.

The door of the house burst open and three children and a teenage boy ran onto the porch and down to the grassy yard, shouting all at once.

Morgan laughed and waved. "Hadley! Diana! Worth!" His voice rang out as he slapped the reins and the horses ran to the yard.

Laurel's heart thudded so loud she was sure Morgan could hear it over the great noise of the horses' hooves and the rattling wagon.

He yelled, "Whoa!" The team stopped near the house and he leaped to the ground and gathered the three children close in his arms. They hugged him and all chattered at once.

The gangly teenage boy stood to one side with a grin on his freckled face and one hand wrapped around the suspender of his faded and patched overalls.

Slowly Laurel climbed to the ground and stood beside the wagon. Were her legs weak from riding or weak from meeting the family that was suddenly hers? She pushed her bonnet off her head and let it settle between her shoulder blades. With trembling fingers she pinned her hair back into a neater knot at the nape of her neck. She smiled at the boy and he quickly looked away, his face red. She studied the children, all too young to attend school. The oldest boy, who looked about six, had the dark coloring of his father. The girl who was four or five and the younger boy, who was probably three, were blond and blue-eyed. Their clothes were rumpled and dirty, their hair long, matted and dirty.

Laurel wanted to introduce herself to the neighbor boy, but she figured Morgan would, so she stood quietly waiting for Morgan to remember her.

A horse whinnied in the corral beside the barn. Chickens clucked and scratched in the dirt beside the sod house. Wind blew a small dust devil across the yard.

Finally Morgan turned to Laurel, the youngest

child high in his arms. "This is my family, Laurel," he said softly. "This guy is Worth. Here's Diana, and Hadley is my oldest. And I won't forget the friend and our neighbor, Johnny, who has watched them for me when I needed help."

"Hello," said Laurel, smiling stiffly.

They stared at her shyly. Only Johnny smiled and said, "Howdy."

"Kids, this is Laurel Bennett. Remember her? We saw her in church. She was the school teacher." Morgan's arm tightened around Worth and he rested a hand on Diana's head. "Laurel has come here to take care of us, to help us. To be your...new ma."

"Hello," said Laurel, but no one answered. The children stared at her with wide frightened eyes. Johnny looked too surprised to speak. "I am very happy to meet all of you." Her voice trailed away and she looked helplessly at Morgan. Suddenly he looked as frightened as the children and she knew she couldn't expect any help from him at this moment. Lifting her skirts a little, she walked to the back of the wagon. "We'll get the supplies and my trunk unloaded and I'll get supper started."

"Yes. The supplies. Let's get to work," said Morgan, standing Worth on the ground. Morgan pulled out the tailgate and slid the supplies forward. "Here, Johnny. Take this to the barn." He settled a sack of grain on Johnny's thin shoulder. "Kids, you go with Johnny and let me show Laurel the house."

A few minutes later Laurel followed Morgan to the house. His boots clomped loudly across the porch. She liked the look of the porch. It would be a fine place to sit in the evening to rest and talk and watch the sun go down. A cactus garden would be perfect along the edge. At the thought of a cactus garden, pain squeezed her heart and she pushed the thought aside. She never wanted to see another cactus garden as long as she lived.

The door squeaked as she opened it for Morgan. He walked in and dropped her trunk on the floor.

"This is the kitchen," said Morgan.

She looked at the big black cast iron range, the oval oak table with two benches and two chairs pushed up to it, a tall white cupboard and a wash stand beside the front door. The floor was made of wide plank boards and looked new. "It's a nice kitchen," she said.

He smiled proudly. "Rachel thought so too." The smile faded and he rubbed an unsteady hand across his eyes. Hoisting her trunk to his shoulder, Morgan strode through the front room where Laurel caught sight of two rockers beside a brick fireplace. He stepped into a spacious bedroom and set her trunk along the wall between two tall windows covered with muslin curtains.

"This is your room," he said. A muscle jumped in his jaw. Pain flickered in his eyes. "We'll unload the wagon while you settle in and start supper."

Before she could speak, he walked out closing the door with a solid click. Slowly she turned to survey the room. A round rug covered part of the plank floor between the big bed and heavy oak dresser. A bright patchwork quilt covered the bed.

The tall headboard and footboard were carved with flowers and leaves. The same design was on the dresser and wash stand and commode. Two faded print dresses and a white petticoat with flowers embroidered on it hung on pegs on the wall next to the dresser. A framed looking glass that stood on curved legs flashed back Laurel's reflection and she turned quickly away. The dusty, haggard-looking woman couldn't really be her. She always had a sparkle in her eye and a smile on her lips. But that was before today, when her sin had been found out.

Slowly she turned to her reflection and shook her finger at it. "You will get back the sparkle and the smile! You will put the past behind you and make the future special."

With a groan she turned away.

The room smelled stale as if no one had opened a window for days.

Slowly Laurel untied her bonnet and dropped it on her trunk. She pulled open a dresser drawer and found it full of women's clothing. A hint of rose sachet drifted out. "Rachel's clothes," she whispered. She closed her eyes and moaned, then carefully pushed the drawer shut. Rachel Clements might be dead, but she still lived here.

Laurel walked to the middle of the room and looked around with her hands on her waist, her mouth puckered and her eyes narrowed.

Was there room enough for her and Rachel both in this family?

CHAPTER 3

In the kitchen Laurel hooked the stove handle in place and lifted the lid. Carefully she pushed in kindling she found in the woodbox beside the cast iron range. She struck a match and dropped it on the kindling. Immediately flames flared and crackled and she adjusted the damper. Smells of sulfur and burning wood filled the air. She rubbed her hands over the bibbed apron that she'd dug out of her trunk. Sounds of voices drifted in through the screen door and she knew Morgan was talking with his children.

"What have I done?" she whispered. She spread her hands wide just as her pa had done many times. "Oh, Pa," she muttered. What was done was done and she wouldn't moan over it. Ma had always said, "Don't cry over spilt milk, Laurel." Oh, how she needed Ma and Pa now!

Sighing, she added small chunks of wood to the fire and put the lid in place. She filled the heavy teakettle with water from the bucket on the washstand beside the door and set the kettle to heat. Grease and dust coated the gray kettle and she knew it would take a hard scrubbing to clean it.

Opening the cupboard, Laurel found the dishes stacked neatly in place. She pulled out a drawer that held silverware and another with sharp knives. She ran her hand over the table and touched the back of a chair. On the surface everything looked tidy and kept up, but she could see the deep-down dirt hadn't been touched in a long time.

Just then Hadley opened the screen door and Morgan walked in with a load of supplies that he set on the floor. The children stood at the door, staring at Laurel without speaking or smiling. She forced a smile but they didn't return it.

"I'll have supper ready soon," she said in a bright voice that sounded too loud.

"I'll show you the pantry and the cellar," said Morgan, pushing back his hat. He glanced toward the stove and the woodbox. "Kids, fill the woodbox."

"Yes, Pa," they said in one voice as they pushed out the door together. Worth looked too small to carry more than a stick.

Morgan hoisted a bag of flour on his shoulder and walked to a door at the right of the stove. "The pantry," he said as he pushed open the door.

She saw rows of canned goods and sealed canisters that she knew held sugar and flour and other things that had to be protected against mice. A lantern stood on the floor beside a door. Morgan opened the door and Laurel saw that it led down steep steps to a cellar. The musty smell drifted up. Morgan struck a match and lit the lantern, then walked down. Slowly she followed. It felt cool, almost cold after the heat of the day.

His shadow danced on the dirt wall. "Here's the potato bin," he said. She looked at the small shriveled potatoes to be used for planting next year's crop. Ma had taught her years ago how to cut planting potatoes into pieces, leaving at least two eyes per piece. The eyes sent out roots that grew into a plant with roots full of new potatoes.

"Here's the cold box," said Morgan as he opened a heavy door built right into the wall. Cold air rushed out and she stooped down to peer inside at butter, milk and eggs.

"I take it you know how to cook," he said.

"Since I was six. I taught Fred's girls." She bit her tongue and looked quickly away as pain stabbed through her. That part of her life was over.

"The sooner you get him off your mind, Laurel, the better you'll be," said Morgan gruffly. He led her back upstairs and she followed slowly, her eyes on the worn heels of his boots and the frayed cuffs of his blue denims.

He stopped in the pantry to turn out the lantern and she almost bumped into him.

Diana ran to Morgan. "Let me turn it out, Pa."

She turned the tiny knob the wrong way and smoke billowed out. The smell of kerosene took Laurel's breath away. Quickly Morgan turned the knob the other way and the flame died down and went out, but the smell hung in the air.

"You can't do nothin' right, Diana," said Hadley.

She hung her head, her cheeks bright red.

"Hadley!" said Morgan sternly.

Hadley ducked his head, but Laurel caught the flash of anger in his eyes.

"Laurel, I'll milk the cow tonight," said Morgan. "Get the pail, Hadley." Morgan turned back to Laurel. "Can you milk?"

She nodded. She'd learned to milk before her hands were strong enough to do a good job. Pa had always finished for her until she had the strength to strip the cow dry.

"Good. I won't have time after this and Hadley still can't do it alone."

"Sure, I can, Pa!"

"Hadley," said Morgan with a frown at Hadley before he turned back to Laurel. "Hadley can milk some, but it'll be up to you to do it. He can help."

Laurel nodded. "I'll be glad for his help." She didn't say that she didn't like to milk, didn't like the smell of the cow or the warm milk. She especially hated when the cow swished its tail and caught her in the face with it.

"You fix supper and the kids and me will go milk," said Morgan. He grinned down at the kids. "Let's go see what old Bessie will give us this time."

Laurel stood at the door and watched Morgan and the children walk to the barn. Diana and Worth had to run to keep up. Hadley hung back, the empty pail bumping against his leg as he walked.

The water boiled in the teakettle and Laurel wadded up the tail of her apron and used it to grab the handle and slide the kettle to the back of the range. Water bounced from the spout and spattered and danced across the hot cast iron. Laurel backed away and smoothed down her apron.

A pleasant breeze blew in through the screen door and she turned toward it and let it cool the sweat on her brow. She smoothed back the damp tendrils of dark hair that had escaped the bun at the back of her neck.

In the pantry she picked up a jar of canned beef, one of string beans and another of carrots. She carried them to the table, opened them and poured them together into a tall pot and set them to warm. She brought several potatoes up from the cellar, peeled them carefully and put them in another pot of water to boil. She saved the peelings to feed the chickens in the morning. The chickens were probably already roosting for the night.

She found flour, baking powder, salt and lard and mixed up a batch of biscuits. Cutting them into rounds with a tin cup, she placed them on a black pan and slid them into the hot oven.

When the potatoes were soft, Laurel poured off the water and added the potatoes to the meat and vegetables. She thickened the broth with flour, making a fine stew. With all the butterflies fluttering inside her, she didn't know if she'd be able to eat at all.

She turned to catch the cool breeze just as Diana opened the screen door to let Morgan in with the pail of foamy warm milk.

"Smells good in here," he said as he handed her the bucket of milk. "The straining cloth and clean bucket are just inside the pantry." He turned to the children. "You kids wash for supper and set the table for your...for Laurel."

Laurel saw the anguish on his face before he turned to fill the washpan with warm water and her heart ached for him. She carried in the clean bucket and two white cloths. Ma had always said it was best to strain the milk twice just to make sure it was clean. Carefully Laurel stretched the cloth over half the top of the foamy warm milk, gripping it tightly along with the bucket of milk. Slowly she tipped the bucket and poured the milk through the cloth into the clean bucket. Foam and dirt and cow hair clung to the cloth. She dropped it in the dirty pail and strained the milk again. She set it in the cold box so the cream would rise to the top. She would use that to make butter. After supper she'd wash the buckets so they would be ready for morning milking.

The children had the table set by the time she finished with the milk. The boys sat on one bench and Diana on another. Morgan sat on a chair at the head of the table, leaving the chair at the foot and closest to the stove empty. It was Rachel's chair. Laurel bit back a groan. She had to sit on Rachel's chair. She knew what the others were thinking. Oh, if only she could turn back time!

In silence she put the food on the table and slowly sank down on Rachel's chair.

Morgan bowed his head and, thankfully, Laurel did too. "Heavenly Father, thank You for all You've provided for us. For all of Your blessings." His voice broke and Laurel locked her hands tightly in her lap. Finally Morgan continued. "Thank You for the good food as well as Your constant protection and love. In Jesus' name. Amen."

He lifted his head and smiled. Laurel could see it took a lot of effort to do it.

Quietly she served the stew and biscuits to Diana and Worth who were too small to help themselves. Hadley and Morgan filled their plates. No one said a word as they ate. Laurel swallowed her food without tasting it. Morgan filled his plate three times and ate six biscuits.

Worth's head drooped and his silky lashes touched his pale cheeks. Laurel pushed back her chair and walked around to him. "I'll tuck Worth into bed," she said. Her voice seemed to boom out into the terrible silence and she flushed.

Worth jerked up and tears filled his wide blue eyes. "I'm not tired," he said as he slid closer to Hadley.

"But you're falling asleep at the table," said Laurel.

"We always read the Bible and pray before we leave the supper table," said Morgan. "After that you can put Worth to bed."

"I won't go to bed," he whispered.

Morgan shot him a look and he ducked his head and was silent.

Laurel sat back on Rachel's chair and folded her hands in her lap as Morgan lifted the big black Bible from a shelf near the table. He opened it and read a Psalm. His voice was deep and pleasant, but Laurel didn't hear what he read as she thought of the many nights that she had sat at her father's table, listening to him read, then later at Fred's table, listening to him. Hearing the Scriptures had always been special to her, but she found herself listening to Fred just to hear his voice, not for the words he read. She bit her lip to hold back the cry of guilt.

"We always hold hands when we pray," said Morgan with a slight catch in his voice. He reached out to Hadley and Diana as Laurel reached out for Worth and Diana. They hesitated, then finally offered her their hands.

"Heavenly Father, we praise You for who You are. We thank You for all You've done for us. We want to please You always and do what You want us to do. Thank you for bringing Laurel into this family." Morgan faltered and Laurel bit her lip. "Make us a blessing to her and help her to be a blessing to us. In Jesus' name we pray. Amen."

"Amen." whispered Laurel. She did want to be a blessing to them. She wanted to help them even though the children didn't want her. They needed her. She would do what she could. Her own happiness didn't matter.

Finally Morgan pushed back his chair and stood. "Laurel, thanks for the supper. It was very good."

"Not as good as Ma's," said Diana with a scowl.

Laurel stiffened.

"Nobody can cook as good as Ma," said Hadley with his head down and little flags of red waving in his cheeks.

Laurel glanced at Morgan.

"Ma was a very good cook," said Morgan softly.

"But Laurel is too."

"Thank you," she whispered. Part of the tension eased and she walked around to Worth. "Show me where you sleep."

He burst into tears and flung his arms around Hadley. "Don't let her touch me! I don't want her!"

Laurel looked at Morgan to know what to do, but his back was turned. She knew he was leaving her to her job. She gently took Worth's thin arm. "I'll help you wash your hands and face, Worth, and then you're going to bed. Come along." She knew she sounded like the schoolteacher she was. Worth cried harder and clung tightly to Hadley.

"Let me go!" said Hadley, pushing against Worth.

"I won't go to bed!" screamed Worth.

Morgan turned and frowned at Worth. "You will go to bed, Worth Clements. Stop the crying! You mind your...you mind Laurel."

Worth sniffed and knuckled away his tears and finally allowed Laurel to wash his hands and face.

"How old are you, Worth?" she asked.

He looked at her a long time, then finally pulled a hand free and held up three fingers.

"You're a fine boy." She wanted to pull him close to her heart, but she dried his face and hands and let him lead her to a closed door in the front room about three feet from her room. Just as she started into his room she caught sight of a piano against the inside wall of the front room.

"You have a piano!" she cried.

"It's Ma's," he said.

From the way he said it she knew that he didn't want her to touch it. She walked away from it and helped him into his nightshirt. It hung on his thin body and brushed the plank floor.

"This is my bed," said Worth. "Mine and Hadley's. Diana sleeps there." He pointed to a narrow cot covered with a small flowered quilt that stood across the room near the window.

Laurel pulled back the quilt on Worth's bed and he just stood there, looking up at her.

Morgan walked in and Worth ran to him.

"*She* didn't know I had to pray," said Worth.

Laurel shrugged. She should've known, but she hadn't thought of it.

"We'll pray with you, Worth," said Morgan.

Worth leaned against the bed with his hands folded and his eyes closed. "Dear God, thank You for this day. Thank You for Pa and for Ma and for Diana and for Hadley. No, not Ma. Ma's in heaven with You. Amen."

Tears clung to Laurel's long lashes and she couldn't look at Morgan.

Worth slid into bed and Morgan pulled the quilt to his chin, then leaned over and kissed his cheek. "Sleep tight, son."

Laurel patted Worth's head. She knew he wouldn't want a kiss from her even though she longed to give him one to help ease his pain.

Morgan walked out of the bedroom and stopped her with a touch on her arm in the front room. "I'll fix a mat on the floor next to the fireplace," he said in a low voice.

"No!" she cried, then whispered, "No. I'll sleep on the floor. I can't let you do that!"

He studied her for a minute without speaking. She saw the tired lines around his eyes. "Laurel, this is hard enough on you as it is."

"And on you!"

With a slight nod he acknowledged that it was. "I'll take the floor. That's settled."

She sighed and nodded. From the look on his face and the sound of his voice she knew he wouldn't change his mind no matter how hard it was on him to sleep on the floor. But more than that, hard on him to have her sleep in the bed that Rachel should be sleeping in, that Rachel had slept in until her death two weeks ago. "It's settled," she said.

"Good." He walked to the kitchen and she followed. "Let's go outside a while, kids," he said as he pulled Hadley and Diana close to his side. "We have to shut up the chickens to keep the coyotes out."

"I saw a coyote today," said Diana as they walked out. "I wanted Johnny to shoot it, but it ran away too fast."

Laurel lit the lamp and set it on the table. She cast a great shadow on the wall and she smiled tiredly. If she'd been at school she would have told a wonderful story about her shadow. The students loved to listen to her stories. She swallowed hard. She was no longer the teacher. Her life had changed, drastically changed.

She blinked back stinging tears as she set the dishpan on the table, filled it with hot water from the teakettle and rubbed soap into it. Hadley and Diana had scraped and stacked the dishes in a neat pile at the end of the table.

In a few minutes the dishes were washed and put away in the cupboard. She poured scalding water into the milk buckets, sloshed it around and poured it into the slop bucket. She sniffed each bucket to make sure even the milk smell was gone, nodded and set one beside the door and the other in the pantry. The milk smell had to be out to keep the morning's milk from tasting bad. She'd known that as long as she could remember.

The screen door squeaked as Morgan opened it and walked in with Hadley and Diana. "You kids wash and get to bed. Laurel and I will be in to tuck you in when you're ready."

Diana peeked at Laurel, then turned quickly away to step on the wooden stool so she could reach the washpan. She splashed water on her face and rubbed dry with a towel. Dirt smeared the towel. Hadley washed next, leaving even bigger streaks of dirt on the towel.

As they walked to their bedroom, Laurel sighed.

"They'll come around," Morgan said softly. "Give them time. They're good kids, but they're hurting mighty bad."

"I know. I just wish I could comfort them but they won't let me."

"It can't happen overnight."

"I know." She trembled with fatigue, suddenly too tired to stand or think or talk. "Is there anything else you want of me tonight?"

"I reckon not." He looked tired too, tired enough to drop where he stood.

"I'll say goodnight then," she whispered.

"I want you to tuck the kids in with me." He rubbed an unsteady hand over his face. "It'll help." He stabbed his fingers through his thick, dark hair. "I won't be around much until the planting is over. You'll be here alone with them."

"I'll manage."

"I know you will."

From the bedroom Hadley called, "We're ready, Pa."

Morgan picked up the lamp and led the way to the bedroom. Laurel thought of all the nights that Rachel had walked with him to tuck in the children and a lump filled her throat. She had been dropped into Rachel's shoes without warning and they didn't fit at all.

She stood beside Morgan and listened to Diana, then Hadley say their prayers. He tucked them in and kissed them goodnight.

In the front room he held the lamp out to her. "You take it. I'll light the one on the mantle."

She took the lamp and felt the warmth from his hand. "I'll fix your mat if you'll tell me where to get the things."

"I can manage." He walked into the bedroom and took a pillow and the quilt that lay folded at the foot of the bed. "Good night, Laurel."

"Good night, Morgan." she said in a weak voice.

She set the lamp on the dresser, hunted in her trunk for her nightdress and quickly undressed and slipped it on. She opened the window and let a cool breeze blow in. Stars twinkled in the sky around the half moon. A horse nickered. In the distance a coyote yapped and another answered. An owl hooted.

Wearily Laurel brushed out her hair and braided it in two braids that hung down her slender shoulders. She bit her lip and frowned. The children didn't want her. "And I don't want to be here," she whispered. She cupped her hand around the lamp globe and blew out the lamp, then stood in the path of light from the window. With her hands locked in front of her she whispered, "Heavenly Father, I need You so!" A tear slipped down her cheek. "I need You and this family needs You." She wiped the tear off with the back of her hand. "Help me. Help me to help them."

From the other room she heard Morgan settle for the night. She let out a long ragged breath. Life was strange.

Finally she climbed into Rachel's bed and pulled Rachel's sheet over her. She felt as if she was sinking, sinking deep into a feather bed. The room seemed to spin like a top but she knew it was because she was tired beyond words.

"Father God, You are so patient with me," she mouthed. "Thank you."

After all the years of sharing a bed with three little girls, it felt strange sleeping alone—strange, but pleasant. She drifted off to a deep sleep. Much later she sat bolt upright, her heart hammering. A child was crying.

She slipped from bed and pushed her arms into her robe. She lit the lamp and held it high as she inched open the door. Morgan was pacing back and forth with Worth sobbing in his arms.

"Can I help?" she asked in a low voice.

He turned to her with a haggard look on his face. "Worth is sick again. He gets this way when he's overtired."

She touched Worth's forehead. "He's burning up. I'll get a cold cloth." She ran to the kitchen, set the lamp on the table and dipped a small towel in the washpan. Wringing it out, she picked up the lamp and hurried back to Morgan. Laurel stood the lamp on a small table between the two rockers. "Sit in the rocker and rock him while I wipe his face and arms."

Morgan sank down and Worth stopped crying to peek at Laurel as she pressed the cloth to his forehead, then rubbed it over him. Each time the cloth felt warm, she wet it again. Finally the fever broke and Worth settled into Morgan's arms and fell asleep.

"I'll take him," she whispered.

Morgan nodded and she eased him out of Morgan's arms and carried him to the bedroom. The room smelled warm and stuffy. She put Worth into bed beside Hadley, then opened the window to let in the breeze. She fixed Diana's cover and tenderly touched her cheek, then crept from the room.

Morgan snored softly from where he sat in the rocker. She hesitated, then draped the blanket over him, picked up the lamp and tiptoed to bed.

Smiling as she slipped between the sheets, Laurel whispered, "I helped tonight. Maybe tomorrow won't be so bad."

CHAPTER 4

Shortly after dawn Laurel balanced on the one-legged milkstool and gripped the pail between her knees. Her skirts brushed against the dirt floor. Pleasantly cool wind blew in the huge door opening. "You ready for this, Bessie?" she asked with a low laugh. Bessie mooed and Laurel laughed again.

With quick, hard squeezes she milked Bessie. The smell of manure and warm milk sickened her and she tried not to breathe. Bessie flipped her tail and Laurel moved enough to avoid all but a few strands of the long hair. "Stop it, Bessie! I don't want that thing in my face this early in the morning!"

She squirted warm milk into the bucket with her head turned and her cheek almost touching Bessie's side. Finally Bessie was stripped dry. Laurel turned her out into the pasture beside the barn. Birds twittered in the trees and a rooster crowed. She had let the chickens out on her way to the barn. Glad to be released, they ran squawking out the door with flapping wings that sent dust flying.

She held the pail away from her to keep from bumping it against her leg as she walked toward the house. Spotting the clothesline, she knew she needed to wash very soon. Laurel groaned at the thought. "Washing, ironing, mending, planting the garden," she muttered. "Taking care of three children. Cooking, cleaning, carrying water, outdoor chores." Noticing the woodpile, she added, "Splitting wood" to the list of all that she had to do.

Inside the quiet house she strained the milk and put it to cool. She found a basket and hurried to the chicken house to gather the eggs and feed the chickens. A rooster flew to the top rail of the corral fence, lifted its red head and crowed loud and long. Laurel laughed. It blended with the other happy sounds around the homestead. A tiny spark of happiness pushed away part of her sorrow. Maybe she wouldn't miss teaching school as much as she thought. And just maybe she wouldn't miss the Saunders family as much as she thought she would either. Her smile vanished and she sighed heavily. She would always miss Fred no matter how far back in her heart she pushed him.

In the distance she saw Morgan walking behind the plow that was pulled by his team of horses. Straight rows of earth piled up and turned over. Birds flew down to grab worms and bugs. She knew that after he plowed, he would disc and drag and harrow, then plant. She had helped Pa work the fields many times while they lived in New York State. The six years she lived in Nebraska she had often heard the arguments about how harmful it was to plow the sandy Nebraska soil. Ranchers who had lived in the area before the homesteaders came claimed the land was for cattle, not fields. One could see the soil blow away in the hot, dry wind, but the homesteaders still continued to plow and to plant and to harvest poor crops each fall.

In the house Laurel changed her apron, washed her hands and pulled out a large bowl to mix up a batch of pancakes. She sifted in flour, salt, baking powder, and a little baking soda. She added eggs and milk and stirred everything into a rich, thick batter.

Several minutes later she had a stack of pancakes ready. She turned to call the children only to find them standing silently at the table, staring at her. All three wore the same clothes they had worn yesterday.

"Good morning," she said, smiling. They didn't answer. "Wash and sit at the table for pancakes. Don't they smell good?"

Without speaking, the children washed their hands and sat in their usual spots. She poured milk for them and helped fix their pancakes. Laurel ate with them forcing herself to talk to fill in the terrible silence.

Finally she pushed back her chair and stood. "Let's go to your room and find clean clothes for you to wear."

"I like this dress," said Diana, tugging at her soiled red and blue flowered calico dress.

"I don't have clean clothes," said Hadley, rubbing the sleeve of his faded blue shirt.

"I want to play," said Worth as he ran toward the door. Laurel caught his arm and stopped him short. He scowled up at her, then his face crumpled and he burst into tears.

"Don't hurt him!" cried Diana, putting her arms around Worth and frowning at Laurel.

"We are going to your bedroom," said Laurel in her firm schoolteacher's voice. "And we're going to see just what we can find."

"A mess is what we'll find," said Hadley as he ran ahead to the bedroom.

She stopped in the doorway. "You're right, Hadley." She laughed and shook her head. "You kids pick up the clothes and take them to the kitchen and we'll wash them." Quickly she folded the quilts and laid them at the foot of the beds, pulled the dirty sheets off the beds and dropped them in a heap. "It looks like this is going to be washday even though it's not a Monday."

They carried the clothes to the kitchen and dropped them in a pile. She stuck wood into the fire. The heat turned her face red. "Now, we'll fill the boiler with water. While it's heating we'll clean the house."

She gave them each small buckets and she took a big one and led the way to the pump. Her arms ached by the time the boiler was full. She sent the children out to play while she swept the floors, dusted the furniture and sorted the clothes into separate piles. For a few minutes she sank down in Rachel's rocking chair, leaned her head back and closed her eyes. Her stomach suddenly growled with hunger. She glanced at the clock on the mantel and she gasped. It was almost noon and dinner wasn't ready!

What would Morgan say if he walked to the house for dinner and found nothing?

Laurel ran to the window to see if he was coming in, but he wasn't in sight. She breathed a sigh of relief.

Suddenly she realized how quiet it was. She heard the crackle of the fire and the hiss of heating water. But she didn't hear laughing and talking from the children.

She ran to the door and called, "Hadley! Children, where are you? Diana? Worth?"

Warm wind blew against her. The sun shone hot from almost directly overhead. Chickens scratched in the dirt. The prairie stretched on and on in front of the house. Laurel ran off the porch and called louder, "Children!"

She looked toward the barn and finally saw the children standing near a fence. Sudden anger boiled inside her. How dare they not answer? She pressed her lips into a thin, straight line as she marched toward the children. Hot wind tugged at her hair and pulled some free from the knot. Her faded dress brushed against the dirt.

She stopped a few feet from the fence with her hands on her hips, her eyes narrowed. Inside the corral a huge bull snorted and pawed at the ground. "Children!"

They spun around, looking very guilty. Worth and Diana pressed close to Hadley, but none of them spoke.

"What are you doing out here? I told you to stay close to the house! Your pa will be coming in for dinner soon!"

"Oh, no!" Diana clamped a hand over her mouth.

"Don't tell him we were here by the bull," said Hadley.

"That old bull won't hurt me," said Worth, kicking toward it.

"It might," said Laurel. "Let's get to the house now. And don't come down here unless I'm with you."

"We can't come down here even when you're with us," said Hadley. "Pa said to stay away from it."

Laurel cocked her brow. "Are you telling me that you children deliberately disobeyed?"

"Not me!" cried Worth.

"You did too," snapped Hadley.

"Please don't tell Pa," said Diana with a worried look. "He'll spank us."

"And well he should!" Laurel shook her finger at them. "You will not disobey or I shall also spank you!"

Handley lifted his chin. "You can't paddle us."

"Oh, yes, I can! Is that clear?" Laurel looked each one squarely in the eyes.

Without another word the children ran to the house. Laurel followed slowly, her legs suddenly tired and her feet sore. In the schoolroom she spent most of her day sitting. Today she'd been on her feet most of the time. Her body would have to get used to the change.

She stepped in the kitchen just as Worth leaped into the pile of dirty shirts. "Stop it!" she cried, hauling him to his feet.

He burst into tears and Diana cuddled him close and scowled at Laurel. "You made him cry. Don't you make him cry again."

Hadley sat at the table with his arms folded, his eyes narrowed.

Her lips pressed together into a straight line, Laurel turned to the stove. It wasn't hot and her heart sank. "It's out!" she muttered as she lifted the lid and clattered it to the range top. Coals glowed brightly and she sighed in relief. She dropped kindling in and watched it catch fire. She criss-crossed larger pieces of wood and dropped the lid in place. Heat turned her face red and made her neck itch under her tight collar.

She shook her finger at the huge pile of clothes. "Just what will I do with this stuff while I fix dinner?"

"Put it in the shed like Ma did," said Hadley.

She stared at him surprised that he'd answered. "What shed?" she asked.

"I'll show you." Hadley ran to the pantry and she followed. He flung open a door that she hadn't noticed before. It led to a lean-to that was attached to the back of the house. A door from the lean-to led outdoors. She glanced around to find two round washtubs hanging on pegs in the wall and a pile of Morgan's dirty clothes half in and half out of a woven bushel basket.

"Thanks, Hadley," she said, smiling. "Children, carry the clothes out here while I make dinner."

While they carried clothes to the shed she rolled out a batch of biscuits and cut them into rounds with a tin cup. She slid them into the oven, made a thick gravy and added a jar of canned beef.

Her stomach growled at the wonderful aroma.

"I'm hungry," said Worth as he pushed blond hair out of his eyes with the back of his dirty hand.

"We'll eat as soon as your pa gets in." Laurel looked out the window, but there was no sign of Morgan riding or walking to the house. Would he expect her to take a basket of food to him like Jane sometimes had for Fred? If so, why hadn't he told her?

"I want to eat," said Diana.

Hadley looked at the gravy. "When can we eat?"

Laurel pulled the biscuits from the oven and set them on the far edge of the stove. "Wash your hands and you can eat now." Would Morgan mind if they didn't wait for him? She considered waiting to eat with him, but she was much too hungry. The biscuits were soft and flaky and tasted good with the beef gravy. The children seemed to like the food too.

Several minutes later she put the children down for naps, then quickly washed the dishes and carried more water to fill the second tub for rinsing the clothes. Perspiration soaked her dress and she unbuttoned the top two buttons and dabbed her prickly skin with a wet washrag. She stepped outside and lifted her chin to let the wind blow against her. But the wind was hot and didn't provide any relief. Wind tugged her hair free of the bun and it fell in hot tangles around her slender shoulders.

Inside again, she braided her hair in two braids the way she had as a girl, then pinned the long braids together at the nape of her neck.

Laurel carried the hot water to the tub in the lean-to a bucketful at a time, whittled slivers from the bar of lye soap into the hot water and dropped in the first load of clothes. She stirred them with a stick to keep from scalding her hands, then when she could touch them she scrubbed them up and down, up and down on the scrub board. Soon her back ached and her hands felt raw. She dropped the scrubbed clothes in the tub of clean, cold water that she'd carried from the well. The cold water felt good against her hands and arms. She splashed cold water on her cheeks and dabbed them dry with the tail of her apron.

The children woke up as she was hanging the clothes on the line. Hot wind whipped wet clothes against her. She hurried to the house and helped them fix leftover biscuits with butter and jelly.

"I need you to fill the woodbox and then you may play outdoors, but you must stay away from the bull," Laurel said firmly.

They nodded and ran out, slamming the screen door after them.

Laurel sighed heavily and walked back to the shed to wash another load of clothes.

The day of work seemed to last forever. Just as she put the last of the clean clothes away, it was time to milk the cow, gather the eggs and fix supper. She listened for Morgan's team, but couldn't hear anything except a coyote yipping in the distance and the children playing in the sand near the porch.

When supper was ready she called the children in and they ate quietly. For the first time she realized just how dirty they were and that it was up to her to see that they got clean. She glanced at the stove and closed her eyes briefly. That meant carrying more buckets of water to heat on the stove.

Later Worth sat in the round tub in front of the range, playing with a cork that she had tossed in for him to use as a little boat. He laughed as he pushed it under the water and watched it bob back up. Hadley and Diana sat at the table drawing on papers with pencils Laurel had dug out of her trunk for them.

Laurel leaned over the tub, rubbed soap onto a washrag, then lathered Worth all over. She knew that if she still lived at the Saunders she would be in her room reading or resting. Would she ever have time to read or rest again?

Finally she lifted Worth out and wrapped a large clean towel around him. She rubbed his hair dry and combed it carefully. His hair covered his ears and eyes and hung down his neck.

"You need a haircut," she said, smiling as she picked up the shears. Suddenly it seemed very strange to be here cutting an unfamiliar boy's hair. Her life was drastically different. Her hand froze in place and she bit her lip to keep from moaning in agony.

"Are you gonna cut my hair?" asked Worth,

peeking through his silky strands.

She managed to smile. "Yes. I certainly am. A lot off here and here." She clipped around his ears and off his neck. Long strands fell to the plank flooring.

"Don't cut him bald!" cried Dianna.

"I won't," said Laurel. "I've been cutting hair a long time. I used to cut my pa's hair. Ma taught me how." She told them a story about the first time she'd cut Pa's hair and how Ma had to straighten it. "Pa thought he was going to be bald," she said with a laugh. "He wore his hat all the time for a long time after that. He didn't want anyone to see his haircut."

She helped Worth dress in clean underwear and a nightshirt. "You are a handsome boy, Worth," she said. "We'll try to keep you clean and smelling good."

He grinned and ducked his head, then sat at the table to scribble while Diana climbed in the tub.

Laurel's back ached by the time Hadley was finished and she emptied the tub out the back door, a bucketful at a time. She tucked the children into bed after they said their prayers, then slowly walked back to the kitchen.

Was Morgan going to work all night long? How could he see? The moon was out, but not bright enough to work by.

She splashed water on her face and neck and wished she could take a long bath. She thought about putting the tub in her bedroom and filling it with water, but she was too tired. Her bath would have to wait until she had more energy.

She left a lamp lit on the table in the kitchen and walked to the front room with another lamp in her hand. She touched the piano, then sat down and ran her fingers lovingly over the keys. The sound of the hymns that she'd played for years rose around her and soothed her. The Saunders didn't have a piano, but she had often walked to the church to play the one there.

Suddenly a strong hand clamped on Laurel's shoulder and she jumped and shrieked, then turned to find Morgan standing over her, his dusty face dark with anger. He hauled her off the stool and snapped, "How dare you touch Rachel's piano?"

"But...but..."

"Do you know how I felt walking to the house and hearing the music that she played, being played on her piano, and knowing that she wouldn't be here waiting for me?"

She saw the anguish on his face as well as the tired lines around his eyes and mouth. "I am sorry if I hurt you."

"Don't ever touch that piano again!"

She narrowed her eyes. "You're being very unreasonable, Morgan."

"You heard what I said," he said stiffly.

She lifted her head and squared her tired shoulders. "I am good enough to wash the clothes, cook the meals, do the chores, take care of your children, but not good enough to have a little enjoyment on the piano? That is not right."

He rubbed a trembling hand over his jaw and his

whiskers sounded raspy. "You can not touch the piano. I'm too tired to argue about it." He stepped around her, lowered the lid on the piano and rubbed his hand over it. He finally turned back to her and she had to bite her tongue to keep back sharp words. "You can put my supper on now," he said hoarsely.

She walked into the kitchen and heated the food, banging the lid against the pot of stew. She carried it to the table just as he sat down. His face and hands were clean and his hair damp. "I thought you'd be here for dinner."

"I took a few biscuits with me this morning." He ate quickly as if he was starving and she sat across from him with her hands wrapped around a cup of coffee. The lamp flickered, casting shadows behind Morgan.

"Do you plan to take food with you every day?" she finally asked.

"Until the planting is done." He drained a glass of milk and poured another from the pitcher. He sighed. "Did you put in the garden today?"

"No."

He looked up with a frown. "Why not?"

Anger churned inside her but she forced it back. "I didn't have time."

"You should have taken time."

"Yes. I should have." She knew she sounded sarcastic, but she couldn't help it. "I'll do it tomorrow."

He nodded as he pushed back his chair. "You'd better turn in. It's late."

She carried his dishes to the dishpan, stacked

them inside and poured water over them. Suddenly the teakettle seemed to weigh more than an armload of wood. "I laid clean clothes for you in the front room on your rocker." She turned and caught an embarrassed look on his face.

"Thank you." he said in a low voice. He cleared his throat and rubbed an unsteady hand over his dusty shirt. "I reckon I forgot how the wash had piled up. That's why you didn't plant today, isn't it?"

She nodded.

"I'm sorry I snapped at you. I'm tired. That's no excuse, but I haven't been myself since...since... Rachel..." His voice trailed off and he turned away, but not before Laurel saw the glint of tears in his eyes.

"You never told me how she...died."

He rubbed his hand around his sun-darkened neck. "Giving birth. Our baby girl died too."

Tears burned Laurel's eyes. "I am sorry," she whispered hoarsely.

He nodded. "Me too."

She walked over to him but didn't touch him. "I am truly sorry about hurting you by playing her piano."

"It's not really her piano anymore, is it?" His voice broke and she wanted to reach out and comfort him. "Play it when you want. When I'm not around."

She touched his arm and he looked down at her hand, then into her face. "In time the pain will go away, Morgan." She knew from experience that it was true, but she could tell that he didn't believe her. "You'll be able to be happy again and live a normal life." She patted his arm softly. "I'll help any way that I can."

He gripped her arms and she bit back a gasp of surprise. "Will you let me hold you and pretend you're Rachel? Will you put your arms around me and kiss away my pain and tell me that you're Rachel come back to me?"

Helplessly she shook her head. "But I can tell you that I'm Laurel and that I am here for you." Her voice was low and full of emotion and tears sparkled in her eyes.

"Oh, Laurel, I want her! I need her!"

"I know." Laurel whispered. She slid one arm around his neck and another around his waist and held him to her. "I know. I know." She felt him stiffen and then he held her tightly and buried his face against her hair. His body shook with sobs and she felt tears slip down her cheeks. He smelled of sweat and leather and fresh-plowed dirt and the soap that he'd used on his face and hands. A strange sensation passed through her, and she held him tightly. Burning wood snapped in the stove and a coyote howled outdoors. The soft glow of the lamp cast long shadows.

Finally Morgan lifted his head and released her. She dropped her hands and stepped back.

"Good night, Morgan," she whispered.

"Good night." His voice was low and hoarse. "Thank you."

She nodded, then walked away from him to the

bedroom that still held all of Rachel's things. She heard Morgan settle in the front room on the pallet beside the fireplace. With a sigh she knelt beside her bed and folded her hands on Rachel's quilt. "Heavenly Father, thank You for filling Morgan with Your peace. Comfort him and help him to sleep well tonight."

She ached with weariness as she continued to pray. A warmth sparked inside her and spread through her and she smiled.

She climbed into bed and closed her eyes. Once again she felt Morgan close to her, their arms around each other and she seemed more fulfilled and more worthwhile than she'd ever been in her life.

In the darkness she smiled and fell asleep.

CHAPTER 5

Hot wind whipping her skirts around her legs, Laurel stepped back from the garden and rubbed the sandy soil off her hands. Finally the last of the garden was in! Two days ago she'd taken the small shriveled potatoes, cut them into pieces, making sure each piece had two or three eyes, spread them out to dry a bit, then planted them in the row she'd made with the hoe.

She smiled as she pressed her hands to the small of her back and surveyed the work she'd done. The garden stretched on and on. It would mean days of carrying water to it when the hot wind blew and the ground was too dry for the vegetables. In the summer and fall she would be harvesting the crops and canning them. She bit back a groan. Somehow she'd manage it all. And as the children grew they'd be able to help. Hadley had helped already and Diana a little. Worth had done more damage than good and she'd sent him away from the garden to chase a young rabbit that he saw sneaking around the sod chicken coop.

Laurel glanced around and spotted the children running in circles, shouting and laughing. They had accepted her much quicker than she thought they would. The first two weeks had been hard, but now they talked to her and called her by name. They couldn't call her Ma yet but she knew it would come in time.

Diana ran to Laurel and tugged on her apron. "Can you make my room now? You said you would when you finished. Are you done with the garden?"

Laurel smiled and nodded. She really was too tired to do another thing, but there was so much that needed to be done that she couldn't quit just because she was tired. "We'll make your room now, Diana. We'll make you the prettiest room around!"

Wind tugged at Diana's white-blond braids and flipped her skirt around her bare legs. "I like you, Laurel."

"I like you, too, Diana." Laurel squeezed Diana's small hand as they walked to the house and to the bedroom. She had already decided how to arrange the furniture to make the room into two rooms. She rubbed the sleeves of her calico dress and retied her apron, then taking a deep breath she pushed the big bed up against the inside wall. Diana helped her shove the dresser next to the door. It fit just as Laurel had hoped it would. She slid a chair to the wall toward the end of the room.

"Here, Diana. You hold the hooks and when I need them, you hand them to me." Laurel climbed on the chair so she could reach the ceiling. Even then she had to stand on tiptoe. With Diana chattering constantly Laurel reached for a hook and screwed it into place, hooked a wire on it, then jumped down and carried the chair across the room. She screwed another hook in place. She had stitched a strip of cloth across the top of a brightly colored quilt and now she threaded it onto the wire. She twisted the wire on the hook and pulled until the quilt hung evenly from the floor. She jumped from the chair and stood back to admire the work, her arm resting lightly around Diana.

"It's so pretty!" cried Diana. She ducked behind the quilt, giggling, then peeked out at Laurel. "My very own room!"

"We'll make a door this way." Laurel pulled the quilt away from the wall just enough to walk through. "And here's how you close the door." She tugged on the quilt and it slid easily along the wire and touched the wall.

Diana's eyes sparkled and she clasped her hands together against her chest. "My own room!"

Laurel pushed the small bed against the wall near the window and slid the humpback trunk to the foot of the bed. She folded Diana's clothes and put them inside. Next she spread a small rag rug at the side of the bed for Diana to stand on to dress or kneel on when she said her prayers.

Wind ruffled the curtains at the window. Sounds of a crow cawing and the boys shouting drifted in.

Diana leaned against the window and shouted, "Hadley! Worth! Come see my room!"

The boys ran inside and looked around. "It's nice," said Hadley.

"I can hide," said Worth, twisting inside a corner of the quilt until only his dirty bare feet were in sight.

A few minutes later Laurel walked to the kitchen to make supper and left the children to talk about whose bedroom was better. Maybe someday Morgan could add on to the house so the boys could have a room to themselves. And Morgan really should have a room so that he didn't have to sleep on the floor. Laurel gripped the teakettle handle tighter. Someday Morgan would share a room with her, a bed with her. She flushed and abruptly pushed the alarming thought aside. She wasn't ready to deal with that. There was still too much to do and too much to think about.

Several days later she walked into her bedroom while the children were taking naps and the house was quiet. She looked around the room, her eyes narrowed in thought. Most of her things were still in her trunk because she was hesitant to touch Rachel's personal belongings. "And Morgan wouldn't want me to," she muttered.

She stared at Rachel's dresses hanging on the hooks, then strode across the room, lifted the dresses off the hooks and tossed them to the bed. "There," she said.

Pulling her dresses out of the trunk, she hung them on the hooks, then stepped back and surveyed them. "There!" she said. "This is my room now."

Laurel glanced at the dresser. A shiver ran down her spine. "Why not? I might as well." She bit her lower lip and just stood there. "I might as well," she said again, her heart thudding hard against the bodice of her cotton dress. This was her room, after all. She had every right to use it. In the three weeks since she came here Morgan hadn't offered to empty out Rachel's things, probably hadn't even thought of it, so she might as well do it herself.

"I will!" She wanted to sound very sure of herself, but the words came out in a croak.

She pulled open the top dresser drawer, then just stood there with her head bowed and her pulse pounding in her ears. Finally she pulled out everything and dropped it on the bed. She opened the second drawer and the third drawer and did the same thing. The bottom drawer stuck a little but she jerked it open, lifted out the contents and added them to the pile.

Lifting Rachel's brush and comb and looking glass set off the top of the dresser, she put her set there.

She relined the drawers and carefully laid her folded clothes inside. With her back to the bed she looked around, then smiled. "There," she whispered. Now it really did look like her room.

What would Morgan say? She trembled.

He hadn't spoken Rachel's name since the night in the kitchen when Laurel held him in her arms and comforted him. Her heart jerked a strange little jerk.

Emptying out Rachel's dresser was probably something she should keep to herself.

She pulled the extra quilts and yard goods from Rachel's trunk. Folding all of Rachel's things carefully, she placed them in the trunk for Diana when she grew up. Almost reverently she put the brush and comb set on top.

Laurel picked up the soft blue yard goods and held it to her. It would make a beautiful dress for her and she really did need a new one. Dare she use it? She squared her shoulders. She was Mrs. Morgan Clements and she could use the material if she wanted! Who would stop her? Surely Morgan wouldn't notice or even care.

She stacked the yard goods in the bottom drawer of the dresser with the blue fabric on top.

A warm breeze blew in the window. A rooster crowed and a horse neighed.

Laurel stood before the tall looking glass and studied her reflection. Her eyes sparkled and her cheeks were rosy pink. She looked happy, actually happy! She leaned closer, her eyes wide in surprise. She smiled. She really was happy living here. It was home. "My home," she whispered to her reflection. "Not Rachel's." She pushed dark strands of hair away from her oval face and pinned them into place at the knot at the nape of her slender neck.

"Laurel," Diana called just then.

"I'm in my room," she answered. "*My* room," she whispered.

The children ran to her doorway, hesitated, then walked inside. She could see that they noticed a difference.

"Did you sleep well?" she asked, smiling.

"I didn't," said Worth. He hated taking naps as much as he hated going to bed at night. "I stayed awake the whole time."

"You did not," said Hadley. "I saw you and you

had your eyes shut and your mouth open and you were sleeping."

Worth ducked his head and grinned sheepishly. "But I didn't sleep long."

"What did you do to Ma's room?" asked Diana as she leaned against the bed and looked around with wide blue eyes.

Laurel moistened her dry lips with the tip of her tongue. "This is my room now, so I put all of your mother's things in that trunk."

Hadley ran to the trunk. "You can't put her things away!" he cried. "You can't!"

"I had to, Hadley. Your mother doesn't live here any longer. She lives in heaven with Jesus. She doesn't care that I packed her things away to make room for mine."

"I want Ma," wailed Worth.

Laurel pulled him close and he let her. "I know it hurts. But she's in heaven and she is happy. She probably knows I'm here taking good care of all of you."

"I'm telling Pa that you packed away her stuff," said Diana, standing with her hands on her hips and her chin high. "He won't let you do it!"

"Your mother doesn't live here," repeated Laurel softly. "I do. I had to make this room really mine."

"This is Pa's room too," said Hadley in a tiny voice.

"I know, but right now it's only mine." Laurel kissed Worth's flushed cheek. "Let's go to the kitchen and have some bread and butter, then you can run outdoors to play."

In the kitchen she sliced thick pieces of bread and spread them with butter that Hadley had churned. While they ate she talked to them about her folks. She knew that they liked to hear stories about when she was a little girl living with her parents.

Later she tied on her bonnet and walked to the garden where weeds and new radishes and beans were poking out of the ground. She smiled. Her first garden! She had helped plant many gardens, but this one was really hers. She hoed out some of the weeds and pulled out others that were too close to her vegetables.

She walked to the edge of the garden and looked out across the waving grasses of the vast prairie. The bright blue sky reached down to the edge of the grass and sat on it like an upside down blue bowl. As far as she could see the land belonged to Morgan. The closest neighbor was several miles away. A cottontail hopped into sight, then quickly away. Honking geese flew overhead in a vee. She knew Morgan was checking his cattle on the range near the creek.

Just then she spotted a prickly pear and laughed in delight, then frowned. When had the pain gone at the thought of cactus? It had gone and she smiled in relief. She'd been so busy since she arrived that she hadn't thought about cactus gardens or Fred much at all.

"I'll start a cactus garden at the house near the porch," Laurel said with a nod. This was her place just as much as it was Morgan's and the children's.

Was that possible? She never had a place of her own aside from what she shared with her parents. This would be her home for the rest of her life.

Maybe someday she would have children running around the yard with Hadley and Diana and Worth. Laurel sucked in air and pressed her hand to her racing heart. Children of her own! Would it really happen? Maybe Morgan would never want to make her truly his wife.

She strode to the lean-to, picked up the shovel and marched to the prickly pear to dig it up. She was not ready to think about becoming Morgan's true wife.

Several minutes later she planted the cactus at the corner of the house with the children looking on. "We'll have a cactus garden here," she said to them, smiling. "Next year it will blossom." She told them how beautiful the blossoms would look and they seemed pleased. "We'll look for more and plant them along this whole area. We can work together to keep the weeds out."

"Ma never had a cactus garden," said Hadley, sounding surprised that such a thing could be if his mother hadn't thought of it first.

"Not everyone likes cactuses," said Laurel, brushing off her hands. She picked a sticker out of her thumb. "Cactus plants aren't always friendly." She laughed and the children finally joined in. "Let's go milk Bessie and get supper ready, shall we?"

After the children were asleep for the night Laurel walked to the front room and sat on the rocker to rest before Morgan came in to eat. She never knew what time to expect him, but each night she sat and talked with him while he ate.

She picked up the big Family Bible that she'd often dusted but never read. Opening it to the family pages, she read the birth dates of the children and the wedding date of Morgan and Rachel. Rachel's death was recorded in a shaky hand. Laurel sighed. Her name had not been written in, nor the wedding date recorded.

With a firm set of her jaw she walked to her room, found her pen and ink and with a flourish wrote down their wedding date and her name with his. Someday someone would look inside the Bible and see that she had indeed been Morgan's wife.

A cricket chirruped in the fireplace. Worth whimpered in his sleep. The lamp flickered.

Glancing at the birth dates again, she realized that Hadley's sixth birthday was only two weeks away. She would plan a special day for him, one that he wouldn't forget. Maybe she could convince Morgan to be home before the children were in bed. Maybe they could have a picnic down by the creek. She needed to buy sugar and candles for the birthday cake.

Weakly she sank to the rocker. Could she go to town and face the people? Had the gossip stopped by now? Maybe Morgan could go to town alone to buy supplies and she wouldn't have to face anyone.

Laurel shook her head. She was not a coward! She would look the school board straight in the eye and let them see that she was a happily married woman with three children to raise. Who then would dare think that she'd considered running off with Fred Saunders?

She closed her eyes and tried to picture Fred, but all she could see was Jane's anguished face as she chopped up the cactus garden.

Laurel groaned. How could she cause anyone so much pain?

The screen door squeaked and Laurel jumped up, her heart fluttering. Morgan was home! She hurried to the kitchen where she had left a lamp burning on the table.

His back was to her as he leaned over the washstand and splashed water onto his face and rubbed his hands around his sun-darkened neck. His clothes were covered with dust and his hair was damp with sweat.

"Hello," she said.

He turned with the towel in his hand, the clean towel she hung over the bar especially for his use. His face was haggard and his eyes bloodshot. "Hi. How're the kids?"

"Fine. Just fine." She filled his plate with food from the warming oven, poured his coffee and sliced thick chunks of bread for him.

As he ate she told him about fixing a bedroom for Diana and he seemed pleased. She couldn't bring herself to tell him about Rachel's things. "Did you find the cattle easily?"

He nodded. "It took a while to find them all, but most of them were near the creek."

"And you're all done planting?"

He nodded.

"That's wonderful!" she cried. "Then we'll be able to be a family again."

His eyes clouded and she wanted to grab back her words. He pushed back his chair and walked outdoors without a word. Slowly she cleared off the table, her movements slow and awkward. Would she ever be able to talk to him without opening a fresh wound?

She heard the back door of the shed open and knew he was getting his clean clothes. He always washed outdoors at the pump, dressed in clean things, put his dirty clothes in the shed and walked to the front room to sit and read the Bible before he fell asleep on his pallet.

A moth fluttered at the screen, trying to get to the lamp on the table. A coyote yapped and another answered.

Laurel filled the dipper with water and drank. She wanted to talk with Morgan. Was he staying outdoors until he thought she'd gone to bed so that he wouldn't have to talk to her?

Finally the screen door opened and he walked in. He was clean and his hair was combed neatly, but he looked ready to collapse with exhaustion. He rubbed his hand over his three-day stubble.

"Good night, Laurel," he said with a slight nod.

"I need to talk to you a minute." Shivers ran down her back and she locked her hands together in front of her.

"Let's go to the front room and sit." He walked ahead of her and sank down in his rocker, crossed his stocking feet and leaned back with a tired sigh.

She unlocked her icy fingers Just what did she want to say? Did she want to tell him about putting Rachel's things away just to see his reaction?

He looked at her, his brow cocked questioningly.

She walked to the piano, rubbed the closed lid and turned to face him. "I found a cactus today and brought it up to the house and planted it."

He nodded but didn't speak. He pushed his fingers through his damp, clean hair.

"I...I put away...Rachel's things." Her heart hammered against the tight bodice of her calico dress. She saw a muscle jump in his jaw. "I needed the space in the bedroom." Still he didn't speak. "It is my bedroom now and I wanted it to look like it."

Why didn't he say anything? She swallowed hard. "I packed her things in a trunk and I'd like you to store the trunk away somewhere."

The color drained from his face and he pushed himself up. "You'd better go before I say something that I'll be sorry for."

She took a step toward him, her eyes flashing. Suddenly she was ready for battle. "Are you implying that I have no right to pack away her things?"

"It's better left alone," he said in a low, tight voice.

"Why is that? So that we can't ever be free of her?"

His eyes darkened with anger. "Free of her? Do you think I want to be free of her? She's my wife!"

Laurel doubled her fists at her sides. "*Was* your

wife. I am now! I live here and I tend your children and I take care of your home and now it's my home and they are my children!" She saw him flinch at her words, but she couldn't stop the wild tirade. "I want to be a part of this home, truly a part of it! Do you know how it feels to have Rachel's things always around me? Nothing really belongs to me. Rachel had it all before I did!"

Morgan shot across the room and gripped her arms and she winced. "This is Rachel's home! Eight years this was her home! I wanted to live with her until we were both old and gray." He shook her slightly. "Don't you step in and push all of her precious memories away! Don't you tell me that those children sleeping in that bedroom are yours. They are not! They belong to me and to Rachel. You are here to take care of them. *She* forced me into asking you!"

Laurel froze and her eyes widened in shock. "Rachel did?"

Morgan dropped his hands and walked back to sit down in his rocker. Laurel stared at him as her legs began to tremble so badly that she couldn't stand. She walked to the small rocker, sank down in it and gripped the arms.

"Rachel knew she was dying." Morgan's voice was almost too low for Laurel to hear. "She knew and she told me that I had to bring home a mother for the children and a wife for...for myself. I refused, but each day I could see her failing and the doctor couldn't do a thing for her. So I stopped fighting. I promised that I would get someone to take her place. She told me that she wanted you."

"Me?" The word hurt her throat.

Morgan nodded. He rubbed a hand across his haggard face. "Rachel said she knew your reputation was spotless and that you loved children. She said you would be a wonderful mother. Finally I agreed."

"I don't know what to say."

He shook an unsteady finger at her. "You have no right to resent her. She brought you here! She said you deserved a home of your own and a family of your own." He gripped the arms of his rocker. "She was too good, too full of love for others, too unselfish. She wanted me to open my home and my heart to you. I told her I couldn't. And I can't!"

Laurel tugged at her tight collar, fighting for breath. Rachel had actually chosen her for this family! Only Morgan didn't want her, had never wanted her even when she thought he had. "So where does that leave us?" she asked in a dead voice. Scalding tears burned the backs of her eyes.

"No different, Laurel," he said tiredly. "I told you before how it was. I didn't tell you about Rachel's part in the whole thing. I only did it now because you seem to resent her and you shouldn't."

"But I can't let her dictate my life! Can't you understand that? I need to be a part of this family for myself!"

"In time, Laurel."

"It'll never happen as long as you keep this place a shrine to her! Don't you see that? She wanted you to bring me here to help all of you, and to help me.

We have to make an effort to make it work. Can't you see that?"

"Are you forgetting your all-consuming love for a married man?"

She fell back, her face suddenly pale. "That is behind me, and you know it."

"Do I?"

"Yes!"

"Can you tell me that you never wish that he was here instead of me? That he was the one you were cooking for or talking to?"

She lifted her chin and looked down her straight nose at him. "I won't discuss such an absurd thing with you."

"And I don't want to discuss Rachel with you."

"But that's different!"

"Laurel, go to bed and leave me alone. I am tired and so are you. We aren't getting anywhere with this."

Slowly she pushed herself up and walked stiffly to her door, then turned to face him. "I still want her trunk out of my bedroom."

He shot from the chair and the rocker rocked back hard. "I see I won't get any rest until I move the trunk. Where is it?"

She led the way and pointed. "There."

He stood beside it and looked around the room at her dresses on the hooks and her things on the dresser. His face hardened and he swung the trunk up on his shoulder and carried it out of the room. She followed him and he lowered it to the floor beside his rocker. He turned to face her, his eyes narrowed.

"Will it bother you too much to have it here until daylight?"

"No."

"Can we have a little peace in this house?"

She wanted to scream or do something drastic to break through the icy barrier he'd built between them, but instead she whispered, "I want peace too, Morgan. But I want so much more than peace."

What was wrong with her tonight? Why couldn't she leave him and walk away from him and sleep alone in the bedroom that she'd made hers? A tear slipped down her flushed cheek and then another. A sob rose in her throat and she choked it back, but a part of it escaped and sounded loud in the room.

Morgan walked to her and softly touched her arm. "Are you crying, Laurel?"

She stood with her head bowed and tears flowing. Finally he lifted her face. She closed her eyes and the tears fell faster.

"Don't cry, Laurel. Please." He rubbed her wet cheeks with his thumbs. "I don't know what you want from me."

"Can you... Do you think you could...could hold me...for a minute?" The words surprised her as much as they did him. But now that she said them she wanted to be close to him, be held by him and feel the closeness they had shared one other time.

A strange look crossed his face, then was gone. "I can do that, Laurel. Yes, I can do that," he whispered. He pulled her close and buried his face in the thickness of her hair.

She leaned against him and wrapped her arms around his waist. The feel of his strong arms around her and his hard-muscled body pressed against hers finally stopped her tears and brought a deep yearning that startled her.

"Feeling better?" he whispered against her ear.

If she moved her head enough so that her mouth was close to his, would he kiss her? The thought shocked her. Did she want him to kiss her? She felt his heart thud against her and she trembled. "I...I am...better," she whispered.

His arms tightened for just a minute and then he held her from him and looked down into her flushed face. "Life is not always easy, Laurel, but God is with us to give us strength. I'm sorry that I can't give you more. In a few days I'll be caught up with my work and I can be part of the family again and make the load lighter for you."

She nodded.

"Go to bed now."

She didn't want to leave him. "Thank you for comforting me when I needed it." She moistened her bottom lip with the tip of her tongue. "A hug can work miracles, can't it?"

He nodded, his eyes hooded. "Good night." He stepped back from her and stood with his feet apart and his hands at his sides. He was tall and lean with broad shoulders and strong muscles in his arms and chest. "Sleep tight."

Laurel turned away and mumbled, "Good night." She closed the door between them and leaned against it, her heart racing and her face flushed.

CHAPTER 6

Perspiration trickled down Laurel's face as she slid the heavy hot iron over the skirt of her best dress. Refreshing wind blowing through the screen door immediately turned insufferably hot because of the blazing fire in the cookstove. Bread baked in the oven, sending out a delicious aroma that made her stomach growl with hunger. Soon the bread would be done and she could let the fire go out until time to make supper.

The iron grew cold and she replaced it with a hot iron from the stove. She wanted to make her dress look its best for their trip to town. Morgan had said they'd go either today immediately after dinner or tomorrow right after breakfast so she could get sugar for Hadley's birthday cake as well as the other supplies they needed. He was checking the fence around the bull. If it didn't need repair, they'd go today. Her stomach tightened and she set the iron on the tripod so she wouldn't drop it.

Did she have the courage to go to town?

She trembled. She couldn't get out of going because Morgan had told the children they could go and he could not manage them on his own.

Finally she picked up the iron and pressed a long strip until it was wrinkle-free. Maybe she wouldn't be the center of attention. She might not see Fred or Jane. She couldn't miss seeing the men on the school board since they owned businesses in town, but she could face them with the children and Morgan.

She held the dress up and frowned at the tiny wrinkles that she couldn't get out around the puffed sleeves. The cotton fabric smelled hot. Carefully she laid the dress over the back of Morgan's chair and picked up his shirt that she'd sprinkled and rolled into the basket. She had been ironing for almost an hour and she wanted to quit.

The aroma of baking bread rose stronger around her and she knew it was time to test to see if it was done. She opened the heavy door and heat struck her. Perspiration rolled down the sides of her face and dampened her dress as she pulled out a pan. The bread was browned and tall. She tapped the top of it just as Ma had taught her to do when she was six and first learned to bake. It sounded hollow and she carefully lifted it out and carried it to the clean white cloth on the table.

She turned it out onto the cloth and walked back for the other loaves. Thankfully she closed the oven, then smeared butter over the top of the bread and left it to cool. Later she would wrap it and put it away.

At the ironing board she licked the end of her finger and barely touched the bottom of the iron. It didn't sizzle and she knew it was too cold. She traded irons and set to work on Morgan's shirt. Her heart fluttered strangely as she realized this was the shirt he wore the other night when he held her close to comfort her.

"Stop it, Laurel," she muttered as she bent to her ironing with a vengeance. Soon she was finished and hung the shirt on her chair.

Just then Worth burst into the kitchen, his face red. "Laurel, come quick!"

"What is it? What's wrong?"

"Hadley. Diana. In the barn!" He plucked at her arm and she ran out the door with him. He stumbled and she swung him up in her arms and ran.

Fear pricked her skin as she felt his tension. She ran inside the big barn and blinked in the dimness.

Worth struggled and she slid him to the hard packed dirt floor.

"Hadley! Diana! Where are you?" she shouted.

"Up there!" cried Worth, pointing.

"Here," called Hadley in a small voice.

"Laurel, help me!" screamed Diana.

Sunlight filtered through the haymow and Laurel spotted the children clinging to the pulley and rope that took the hay to the mow. The rope had stopped swinging and the children were too light to make it swing back for them to drop to the hay on the mow floor. Laurel gasped, her hand at her throat. "Hang on, kids! I'll get you!" She bent down to Worth. "You stay here out of the way!"

Trembling, he nodded.

She ran to the ladder and scrambled up, her skirts tangling around her long legs. Dust tickled her nose and she sneezed. Pulling herself into the mow, she looked around for the part of the rope she could reach. Piles of old hay stood here and there. A mouse ran across the floor and dove out of sight. Laurel bent down and, stretching out her arms, she scooped and pushed piles of hay to the center of the mow. Diana's sobs grew louder. Laurel ran to the wide window and spotted an end to the rope. She grabbed it. It felt rough and big in her hands. "Hang on tight, kids. I'm going to pull the rope and swing you back over here so I can catch you."

"I'm gonna fall!" screamed Diana.

"No, you are not!" Laurel used her school-teacher's firm voice. "You are going to stop crying and you are going to hang on tighter." Laurel yanked on the rope and finally got it to swing until the kids started swinging too. Her heart lodged in her throat as she watched them dangling down from the rope. If they let go they'd fall all the way down to where Worth stood. She shuddered just thinking of it. "Help them, Lord," she whispered as she swung even harder. "When I say let go, let go!" she called to them. She ran to the center of the mow and, when they were right over her, she shouted, "Let go! Let go *now*." She held her arms up to them and they both hit her at the same time and knocked her to the hay with a dull thud. She lay there with the children on top of her, the breath knocked from her body. Hay stuck in her hair and poked through her clothes. "Thank you, Jesus," she whispered.

"Are you hurt?" asked Worth as he poked his head through the hole that led to them. "Are you hurt, Ma?"

Laurel heard him call her Ma and her heart leaped.

Diana jumped up, her fists doubled at her sides. "She's not our ma, Worth, and don't you dare call her Ma!"

Worth ducked out of sight and climbed down to the barn floor, then shouted up, "I want to call her Ma and I will if I want!"

Laurel painfully pushed herself up to a sitting position. Diana and Hadley stood near her feet, their eyes wide. Looking steadily at them, Laurel tugged hay from her hair and brushed dust off her arms. "Come on up here, Worth." she called in a no-nonsense voice. She waited until he stood trembling at her side, his face red. "I want you to call me Ma, Worth." He smiled and looked pleased with himself. She turned her eyes on Hadley and Diana. "I think it is time that you all call me Ma. I just saved your lives. I cook your meals and wash your clothes and read to you and pray with you and even play with you. I deserve to be called Ma. I *am* your ma! Remember that!" She saw the stubborn look on Diana's face and she ignored it. "We're a family now and I want us to act like it." She spread out her arms and laughed. "Look at me. Who else will call me Ma if you three don't?" She laughed harder and finally they joined in. She reached for Worth and he fell into her arms. She tugged on the bottom of Diana's dirty dress and Hadley's pant leg. "Come on, you two. Give your new ma a hug and a kiss."

They looked at each other, then fell down onto her, giggling as she hugged all three of them tight.

"Ma," said Hadley. He pulled away and turned a somersault, laughing as he fell into a pile of hay.

Diana looked at Laurel thoughtfully, then kissed her cheek. "Ma," she whispered.

Worth touched her cheek. "Ma."

Tears filled Laurel's dark eyes and sparkled on her thick, dark lashes. "We certainly turned that frightening situation into a precious memory," she said.

Several minutes later she climbed down the ladder after the children and walked out into the bright sunlight. To her the sky looked bluer and the rooster crowed louder. She laughed.

"Somebody's coming," said Hadley, pointing toward the trail that led to the homestead.

Laurel shielded her eyes with her hand. "Who do you suppose it is?"

Hadley gasped and Laurel looked down at him in alarm. "It's Mr. Stone," he said gruffly.

"Nick Stone?"

"Do you know him?" asked Hadley, frowning at her.

"Yes. Not well, but I know him." And she didn't like him any more than Hadley did. He was a big-time rancher who liked his own way.

"He's mean," said Diana.

"He wants to buy our place," said Hadley. "Pa won't sell to him no matter what. He said so."

Suddenly she realized how she looked. "Kids, we can't let him see us like this! There's still time to clean up a little." She ran to the pump to wash away some of the dirt on her face and hands and helped the kids do the same. She grabbed the towel from the bench near the pump and dried off, then tried to brush the stray strands of hair off her hot face.

As the buggy drew nearer, butterflies fluttered in her stomach. Would Nick Stone know that she was no longer the schoolteacher, but was now Morgan's wife? The last time she saw him he had ridden to the school through the waist-high snow to ask if he could pay court. That was about six months ago. She had outright refused and he said he would do everything in his power to make her life miserable. He hated rejection, especially from a lowly schoolteacher who should have bowed and scraped to him. "You're nothing but an old maid who will grow fat and bitter as the years pass," he had barked at her. "I am the best prospect for a husband around these parts! And you know it."

His words rang in her ears and she wanted to run to the house and hide, but she stood her ground with the children at her side. She watched the black buggy pulled by a matched pair of bays stop several yards from where she stood. Would he be angry enough when he learned that she was married to Morgan that he would hurt the children? She frowned. What could he do? She would not allow him to harm them!

The buggy swayed as Nick Stone stepped out. He was a tall, large man dressed in a gray suit with a string tie and a wide-brimmed hat that covered his salt and pepper gray hair. A heavy mustache almost covered his thick top lip. He reached up and helped a woman from the buggy. She was of medium build and wore a dark blue dress and matching bonnet with black gloves and shoes. Laurel had never seen her before. Nick walked beside the woman toward Laurel and stopped mid-stride when he recognized her. His blue eyes turned to chips of ice. He doffed his hat.

"Laurel Bennett, this is a surprise." His deep voice was harsh.

"Hello, Nick," said Laurel as she slipped an arm around Diana and the other around Hadley. Worth pressed against her skirts. "What brings you way out here?"

He brushed his thick mustache with the back of his hand. "I was taking my sister for a ride and figured I'd stop in and say howdy to the Clements family and give them my regrets about Rachel's passing."

Worth pressed his face against Laurel's leg and she felt him shiver.

"Morgan is gone right now," said Laurel.

The woman frowned at Nick. "You're forgetting your manners, Nick," she said.

"Yes. Yes, Nelda." He rested his long arm lightly on her shoulder. "Laurel Bennett, my sister, Nelda Stone Ross. She's staying with me since her husband died."

"I'm glad to meet you, Laurel," said Nelda with a slight smile. "My brother has talked about you."

Laurel glanced at Nick, then back to Nelda. "My name is Clements now. Mrs. Morgan Clements. I married Morgan in March."

Nick's face darkened with anger, but he masked it immediately. "You did, did you? You said you were happy teaching."

"I changed my mind," she said stiffly.

"And you chose this?" He waved a hand to take in the children and the homestead.

She knew he wanted to say, "You chose this over what I had to offer?" She lifted her chin a fraction. "I'm happy here, Nick." She knew she should invite them in to sit and eat, but she thought of her messy kitchen and she just couldn't. She motioned to the pump. "Could I get you a drink of cold water?" She turned to Hadley. "Water his team, Hadley."

"Don't touch them!" snapped Nick as Hadley stepped forward. He cleared his throat. "They are too spirited for the boy."

"I'd like a drink," said Nelda, patting her cheeks with her handkerchief. "It's hot today and I am thirsty."

Laurel asked Hadley to pump the water while she held the dipper under the spout. Cold water streamed out and she filled the dipper and handed it to Nelda.

"I came on business with Morgan, Laurel," said Nick crisply.

"He doesn't want to see you," said Diana, her face red and her fists doubled at her sides.

"Diana!" Laurel shook her head and frowned slightly. "I am sorry, Nick."

"Bad-mannered child," snapped Nick.

"She is very well-mannered," said Laurel.

Nick pushed his hat to the back of his thick hair and studied Laurel. "While I'm here I want to take a look at Morgan's new bull. I hear it's good stock."

"You stay away from Pa's bull," said Hadley.

Laurel frowned at him, but he wouldn't back down. Finally she said, "Nick, when Morgan returns he'll show you the bull."

Sparks flew from Nick's eyes. "And if he doesn't get back this afternoon?"

She shrugged.

He grabbed Nelda's arm and tugged her toward the buggy. He said over his thick shoulder, "You tell Morgan I'll be back. I hope he knows what he got himself into when he married you, Laurel Bennett!"

"I know very well," said Morgan.

Laurel turned with a gasp. Just how long had Morgan been there?

He smiled at her and slipped an arm around her waist as Nick stared at them. "Nick, I'm sure you didn't come all the way over here to discuss my wife."

"He wants to see the bull," said Worth.

Laurel shot him a look and he closed his mouth and ducked his head. He knew he wasn't to speak unless he was spoken to.

Morgan narrowed his eyes thoughtfully. "Why don't we walk over to the corral and take a look at him? But I'm warning you ahead of time, Nick, he's not for sale. Not at any price. But I'm willing to talk about breeding prices." Morgan dropped his hand and walked ahead with Nick. Laurel felt the empty place on her back where his arm had been and she wished that he'd kept it there.

At the corral they leaned against the fence all in a row like blackbirds, Laurel thought with a grin.

"I'll offer you double what you paid for the bull," said Nick, his eyes on the huge bull grazing several feet away.

"Not even fifty times what I paid," said Morgan. "I need that bull for my place to improve my stock. You already have strong bulls at your place. What do you want with mine?"

Laurel listened with half an ear as they talked about their cattle. She peeked sideways at Nelda to see her reaction to the conversation only to find her staring openly at Morgan with a look that meant more than a casual interest. Laurel frowned and sudden anger flared inside her. Did the Stones think they could have everything they wanted? Surely Nelda was a good ten years older than Morgan.

Laurel bit the inside of her lip to keep back a sharp remark. She'd be glad to see the Stones drive away, hopefully never to return.

Later Nick stopped beside his buggy and turned to Morgan. "I didn't congratulate you yet on your new wife." He smiled at Laurel and she flushed. "She's a fine figure of a woman, and smart too. You got yourself a teacher for your kids as well as a wife for yourself. Quite a smart move on your part, Morgan."

Laurel saw a muscle jump in Morgan's jaw, but he smiled and slipped his arm around her again.

"We're happy," he said.

"Yes, we are," said Laurel, leaning her head against Morgan's arm. She felt him tense, but she didn't think Nick noticed.

"Let's head out," said Nick briskly. He helped Nelda up into the buggy, then climbed in beside her. "Morgan, if you change your mind, let me know." He glanced toward the corral, then at Laurel and she knew the words had a double meaning. He tipped his hat, slapped the reins on the bays and drove away.

"I don't like him, Pa," said Hadley.

"Me neither," said Worth.

"He's not a very nice man," said Morgan as he stepped away from Laurel. "But let's forget about him for now and get dressed to go to town."

The children shouted and ran to the house. Laurel walked slowly along beside Morgan. She felt different somehow, as if she suddenly belonged and she smiled.

"I'm glad you came when you did," she said without looking at him.

"That man has a real hate for you, Laurel. Why is that?"

She hesitated and finally turned to meet his look. "He wanted to...to court me and I said no." She grinned. "He's too mean and he's too old."

Morgan nodded, his face grim. "He'd better not make trouble for you. I almost threw a punch at him when I first walked up, but then I figured I could handle him without hitting him into next week."

She hid a smile as they walked to the door. He

stopped her before they stepped up on the porch. "I'm glad you didn't let him court you."

Her heart fluttered. "So am I."

Morgan smiled and she smiled back. She walked up on the porch with him close behind her. She could smell his dust and sweat and feel the heat of his body and she trembled. For one wild minute she wanted to turn around into his arms and have him hold her just because she was his wife and he was her husband. But he walked around her and picked up the shirt she'd ironed for him and the moment was gone.

"You'd better look at yourself in the looking glass before you start to dress, Laurel," he said with a grin as he pulled a piece of hay out of her hair, then studied her as if it was the most important thing in the world for him to do.

She flushed. "We were...playing in the haymow."

"I should've been there," he said with a low laugh.

Several minutes later she sat beside Morgan on the high seat of the wagon and glanced at the children in the back. They were laughing and talking about the candy they'd buy if they each got a penny to spend.

She retied her bonnet, glad for its shade against the hot sun. A jackrabbit bounced across the trail in front of them. She watched it until it was a speck on the endless prairie.

Just how would the townspeople react to her today?

She locked her hands in her lap and forced back her thoughts of the people. Hadley needed a new pair of shoes and Diana needed yard goods for a new dress or two since she was outgrowing her others. Would Morgan have enough money to buy all they needed? She glanced at him thoughtfully. She didn't know if he had plenty of money or if his pockets were bare. Cash money was hard to come by for most homesteaders. She needed to know before they reached the store. She turned to look at him openly only to find him studying her. He looked away quickly and she thought she detected a slight flush on his face. A tingle ran down her spine and for a moment she was at a loss for words.

The wagon swayed and the harness creaked and jangled. The children named off all the things they wanted to see in town and all they'd buy if they could.

"Morgan?" Laurel asked hesitantly.

He glanced at her.

"Hadley needs shoes and Diana needs goods for a dress and there are other things I need. Is there money for it all?"

He was quiet for a while as he worked the reins with his gloved hands. "I think so." He named the sum of money that she could spend and she nodded.

"That'll do it, but I'll be careful," she said.

"Thank you. Buying the bull left me short of cash. But he will make back all and more than I spent on him."

"Good." She smiled. "I'm glad you didn't sell him to Nick Stone."

"He's a hard man," said Morgan. "He wants my place because of the water on it. He says by rights it should be his, but it is mine, free and clear. Last year I paid off the bank note and I don't mean to take out another." He told her about getting the homestead and adding sections to it, including the one with the lake that Nick said was his. "His cattle watered there for years but he never made a move to make the place legally his. I did, so it's mine. Rachel and I were finally making it pay off." His voice died away and Laurel saw the pain on his face before he turned to look across the rolling hills.

Just then Hadley and Diana started arguing and Laurel turned to settle the squabble. When she turned back, she couldn't start another conversation with Morgan. She knew he had suddenly remembered Rachel and pain had filled him again. Maybe for a while he'd pretended that she was Rachel. Or maybe he'd realized how good it felt to talk to her and had suddenly felt guilty about it. Laurel gripped her drawstring purse tightly. Would he feel disloyal to Rachel if he enjoyed her? Laurel closed her eyes and tried to push back the sudden loneliness she felt.

Midafternoon Morgan stopped in front of the general store, watered the team and looped the reins over the hitchrail. Before he could help Laurel down, she jumped lightly to the ground and helped the children down. She felt the eyes of the townspeople on her and lifted her chin, squaring her shoulders. Her dress fell in graceful folds to her shoes. Her bonnet covered her hair and partly shielded her face.

Arly Larkin stepped outside the hardware store, his head bare and his jacket off. "Morgan. Laurel," he said gruffly. "Brought the youngsters I see."

Laurel could feel the questions buzzing inside Arly's head as she nodded to him.

"How are you, Arly?" Morgan said as he shook hands with him. "Warm day."

"Children, say hello to Mr. Larkin," said Laurel. She watched proudly as they politely spoke to him. "Hadley will be attending school in the fall," she said as she watched Arly closely. "You do have a teacher lined up, don't you?" She saw him flush and she smiled.

"We'll find one," he said stiffly. "But if we don't, maybe you'd help us out for a while."

Laurel started to answer, but Morgan said, "My wife is much too busy to take on the school again. You'll just have to find yourself another teacher. But you'll have to go some to find one as good as Laurel."

His words wrapped around her heart and she smiled. "My husband is prejudiced, of course, Arly. But he is right about my being too busy to teach. Being a wife and mother is a full-time job. Ask your wife. She should know." Everyone in town knew that Arly was a strict taskmaster and kept his wife with her nose to the grindstone.

With a low mumble and a red face Arly walked back inside his hardware store and Laurel followed Morgan into the general store. She fitted Hadley with a pair of shoes and picked out fabric for Diana as well as goods for a shirt for Morgan. Worth stayed near the jars of candy, trying to decide which one to spend his penny on.

Later, outside the store, Laurel touched Morgan's arm and said, "I'd like a few minutes to go to the newspaper office to speak to Ganny Blake if you don't mind. I didn't get a chance to talk to her when I...left town."

Morgan nodded. "Don't be long, though. We have to start back within the hour." He turned to the children. "We'll go to the hardware store and then come back and pick out the candy you want."

Laurel walked away, her drawstring purse swinging from her wrist. Coming to town hadn't been as bad as she thought it would be. She turned the corner and walked right into Jane Saunders. Laurel gasped and stepped back, her face red as shivers ran down her spine. "Hello, Jane," she whispered.

"How are you, Laurel?" asked Jane in a weak voice.

"Fine. And you?"

"Fine." Jane's eyes were sunk back in her head as if she'd been sick.

"The children?"

"Fine." She gave Laurel a look that dared her to ask about Fred.

"I'm on my way to see Ganny Blake and I'm in a bit of a hurry. My husband is waiting." Laurel stressed the word husband and she knew Jane noticed.

"Don't let me keep you." said Jane, lifting her skirts slightly to walk around Laurel to turn the corner.

Laurel's legs trembled and she leaned weakly against the side of the building. Poor Jane. Taking a deep breath, Laurel continued on her way. As she walked past the dentist's office, a hand gripped her arm and pulled her off the street and between the two buildings. She gasped and looked into Fred's haggard face.

"I had to talk to you," he said urgently. "I saw you drive in with Morgan."

She leaned toward him, her heart racing.

"I can't go on like this! Do you know how much I miss you?"

All the love that she'd felt for him surged back and she gripped his hand as tears filled her dark eyes. She forgot her marriage to Morgan and how wrong it was to love Fred. "I will always love you!" she whispered passionately.

"Then why did you marry Morgan Clements? Why?"

"It was the only way out," she whispered brokenly. She wanted to creep into his arms and stay there forever.

"Laurel," he whispered. He gathered her close and she lifted her lips for his kiss when a sound behind her startled her and she turned her head to find Morgan standing there, his eyes blazing. Blood pounding in her ears, she broke away from Fred.

"Keep your hands off my wife," said Morgan savagely as he pulled Laurel to his side. "Never touch her again or I'll knock your teeth down your throat."

Laurel touched Morgan's arm. "Don't. Please don't," she whispered.

"Quiet!" He glared at her and words died in her throat. He turned to Fred. "Your wife is looking for you. For her sake I hope she doesn't learn about this meeting."

Fred jerked his hat low on his haggard face and strode away. Laurel wanted to call after him, but she bit back the words. A tear slipped down her ashen cheek and splashed onto Morgan's hand.

He gripped her arm. "Dry those tears! He's not worth crying over." He pushed his face down close to hers. "I should've known you were coming here to meet him. You had no intention to talk to Ganny Blake!"

His words stung her and she lifted her head and faced him squarely. "But I did! I didn't know Fred would be here."

"I saw them drive past the general store earlier and I'm sure you saw them too. Don't lie to me, Laurel!" His face was grim and she could feel the anger burning inside him.

Her shoulders sagged and she bent her head. "Let's go home. You won't listen to me nor believe anything I say."

"I know what I saw," he snapped as he guided her back to the plank walk. "I hope no one else saw the two of you."

Her body burned with embarrassment at the terrible thought.

He stopped her before they turned the corner. "Smile, Laurel," he said grimly. "Smile at me and laugh. We're going to the wagon where the kids are waiting and we're going to look like a happy family. Do you understand?"

She nodded and blinked away the scalding tears of shame.

He bent down to her. "You'll do it for us and for the Saunders family. Now, smile!"

She lifted her head and smiled as they walked to the wagon. People spoke to her and she spoke back in a cheerful voice, but she didn't know what she said. Morgan helped her up onto the high seat, then he sprang up beside her. Tension crackled between them and she wanted to move away from him, but she sat very still with her hands folded over the purse in her lap.

He clucked to the horses and drove away from town and out onto the prairie. The children sat quietly in the back as they licked their candy sticks. Morgan stared straight ahead, his face set.

Laurel looked toward the rolling hills, her eyes dry and her heart heavy. Her back ached from sitting so stiff, but she couldn't relax beside Morgan.

He probably hated her now, hated her and wished that he'd never married her. He would never trust her again. He would never hold her close to comfort her no matter how badly she might need it. She had ruined everything in that brief moment with Fred.

It had not been worth it. The realization took her breath away, but she knew it was true. Could she ever convince Morgan of that?

CHAPTER 7

Laurel glanced up at the sky as thunderclouds rolled across the morning sun and blocked out its hot glare. Lightning flashed in the distance. She gripped the hoe tightly and bent to chop the weeds from the flourishing garden. She was only half done and had already been working for an hour. How she hated weeding the garden! She had put it off the past few days until she saw Morgan looking at it this morning before he rode out to check on the cattle on the north range. He didn't say anything about the weeds but seeing his face, she knew what he was thinking.

She swung the hoe so hard she nearly chopped off a bean plant. The milkweed flew almost over her head. Why couldn't she chop her troubles away as easily? Since their trip to town six weeks ago Morgan had talked to her only when it was necessary. Around the children he treated her politely and even managed to smile at her, but when they were alone he was abrupt and often sharp and at times didn't speak at all. "I don't blame him a bit," she muttered as she chopped at another milkweed. She deserved what he was giving her even though she had apologized and he said that he forgave her. She knew it was as hard for him to forgive her as it was for her to forgive herself. She read 1 John 1:9 that said if she confessed her sin, Jesus was faithful and just to forgive her sins and cleanse her from all unrighteousness. She was forgiven no matter how she felt!

She knocked a tomato worm off the vine and squashed it in the sand. The green slime turned her stomach and she looked quickly away.

Why had she fallen into Fred's arms? How could she still love him when she knew it was wrong?

She groaned and shook her head. Thunder rolled and she jumped.

"Ma!" shouted Diana, running around the house with the boys behind her. She caught at Laurel's hand. Her eyes were wide with fright. "It's gonna rain!"

"I'm not scared," said Worth, pressing close to Laurel.

"Go play in the barn with your kitten," said Laurel. Abigail Lasco had brought over a little black kitten with a white paw for them last week. They named it Kitty. "And stay off the rope and pulley!"

"We will," said Hadley as they all ran toward the barn.

Laurel leaned on her hoe and smiled as she watched them. Wind almost blew them off their course. "I love them so much!" she whispered fiercely. She knew they loved her. Never had she expected to have such feelings for children. She had cared about her students, but this was very different.

She remembered the fun it was to make a birthday cake for Hadley and to have a special party for him. Morgan had joined in and she knew what a strain it was on him. She frowned. Life couldn't stop just because she had made a terrible mistake, and not even because Rachel had died early. Morgan had to realize that and get on with living.

Thunder boomed closer and Laurel turned to scan the prairie. Would Morgan ride to the house to take shelter?

Her heart lurched at the thought of seeing him and she gripped her hoe and bent over the next row, chopping as if her life depended on it.

Perspiration soaked her clothes and ran down her face, burning her eyes. Scorching hot wind flipped her bonnet around on her back, caught at her hair and tugged strands free from its knot. She struggled to breathe the oppressive hot air. Finally she stopped hoeing and gasped for breath. She would have to finish the garden after the rain.

Wind whipping her skirts around her legs, Laurel ran to the pump and pumped out cold water to splash on her face and neck and hands. Sand swirled around the yard. The chickens squawked and ran for the coop. Suddenly the wind blew stronger and almost knocked Laurel off her feet. She looked at the sky and her heart lurched. A bad storm was coming and would hit soon.

"Hadley! Diana! Worth!" she shouted with her hands cupped around her mouth. The wind blew her words back against her. She bent into it and ran toward the barn. Lightning snaked across the dark sky and thunder boomed just as she ran into the barn. Diana screamed in fear and fell against Laurel.

Laurel balanced Worth on her left hip and held Diana's hand with her right hand. "Hadley, hold on to my apron and don't let go no matter how hard the wind blows or how fast we run."

His face white, Hadley gripped her apron tail. "I'm ready," he said.

"Run fast!" shouted Laurel. She ran toward the house with sand whirling around her, stinging her face and arms. Diana stumbled, but Laurel hauled her up and kept running. They ran up on the porch and she released Diana to open the screen door. She fought against the wind and finally opened the screen enough for Hadley and Diana to run inside. Wind tore at the screen almost jerking it from Laurel. She pushed Worth inside and struggled with the screen as she slipped inside and latched it shut.

"That was close," she said, panting hard.

Suddenly great drops of rain hit the house. "The windows!" she cried. "Hadley, get that one." She pointed to the kitchen window, then ran through the house, closing windows with a bang. She walked back to the kitchen and stood at the window with the kids to watch the wind and rain. The temperature dropped rapidly and the house creaked as it cooled off.

"Pa's gonna get awful wet," said Diana.

"Do you see him?" asked Laurel, trying to see through the rain. It poured so hard that she couldn't see past the porch. Just then the wind whipped the rain enough that she saw the chicken coop door swing back and forth. She would have to close it before it tore off the hinges and the rain soaked the chickens.

"Where is Pa?" asked Worth with his nose pressed against the pane.

"He'll be all right," said Laurel.

"He might get blowed away," said Diana.

"He's strong," said Hadley.

Laurel pulled her hair back and tied it with a string. "Kids, I must go lock the chicken house door. Stay right here and don't run out after me." She bent down to Worth. "Do you hear me, Worth? You stay with Hadley and Diana."

He nodded.

"He will," said Hadley in a voice that meant he'd better or else.

Laurel smiled at Worth and he smiled back. "Be right back, kids." Taking a deep breath she eased out the screen door and ran off the porch. Cold rain soaked through her clothes to her skin before she reached the chicken coop.

She wrestled with the door, closed it, locked it and leaned there for a while to catch her breath, then ran back to the house. Inside, rivulets of water streamed from her skirts to the floor. She grabbed the towel off the washstand and dried her face. "I am *so* wet!" she gasped, laughing.

Diana pushed a big towel into her hands and she wrapped it around her shoulders.

"I wish Pa would get home," said Hadley,

peering out the window again.

"He will," said Laurel. Had he found shelter? What if lightning had struck him? What would she do without him? Her stomach knotted and she forced the fearful thought aside. "Your pa will be just fine. God is with him," she said.

"God takes care of all of us," said Diana.

"He does," said Laurel with a smile. "I have to change my clothes. You kids sit down and cut and paste here at the table while I do." She laid out the things, then walked to the lean-to and pulled off her wet clothes, toweled dry and slipped on the clean shirt that she'd put there for Morgan. The shirt hung below her knees and she laughed. What would Morgan say if he saw her now? Her nerve ends tingled just thinking about it.

Laurel hurried to her room and dressed in dry clothes that felt soft and warm and comfortable against her cold skin. She brushed her damp hair and left it hanging down her shoulders and back like a glossy brown blanket. She pulled on her stockings and good shoes and walked to the kitchen just in time to stop Worth from eating the flour and water paste.

"Let's clean up here and go sing at the piano," she said brightly. "It'll chase away all the gloom."

In a few minutes she sat at the piano and the children stood beside her. She played the songs she had taught them to sing and they sang with gusto. Hadley had a good voice and sang out boldly.

Diana remembered all the words, but often sang off key. Worth usually forgot the words and made up his own as he went along.

Later she made dinner, hoping Morgan would return to eat, but they ate without him. The fire in the stove took the damp chill off the room. She glanced out the window as often as she could without worrying the children. They helped her with dishes and she put them down for naps. Hadley felt he was too old for a nap now that he was six, but she had him rest anyway.

As they slept she paced the kitchen, praying under her breath for Morgan's safe return. She pushed her hair out of her face and back over her shoulder. Suddenly she remembered her pile of wet clothes in the shed. "I'd better hang them to dry," she muttered as she walked through the pantry and into the shed.

Just inside the shed door she stopped with a strangled gasp. Morgan lay in a crumpled heap on the floor over her clothes. He was covered with mud and blood. The room spun and her ears buzzed. What had happened to him?

She dropped down beside him and touched his dirty face and his bloody arm. She saw his chest move and sagged in great relief. "Morgan," she whispered. "Morgan!"

With trembling fingers she unbuttoned his shirt and pushed it open. Dark hair curled on his chest, but she found no wound. Where had all the blood come from?

His eyelids fluttered and he looked at her, his

eyes glazed with pain. "Laurel."

"What happened to you?"

He struggled to sit up and she held him as if she'd never let him go. He leaned his head against her breast and her pulse leaped.

"Help me to the kitchen," he said. His voice was low and weak and tore at her heart.

Her legs trembling, she stood, then bent to him. He struggled to stand and leaned heavily on her. "Can you make it?" she asked.

He nodded slightly, but she could see by his drawn face what an effort it was just to stand.

Staggering under his weight, she managed to walk him to his chair in the kitchen. She eased him down, than gasped as blood gushed from his muddy right arm. "Oh, Morgan! Your arm!" She slid his shirt off and winced when he did. "What happened to you?" She dabbed at the blood with the shirt.

"Lightning almost hit me and my horse spooked. He bucked me off into a couple of scared cows with long horns."

"You poor man!" She examined his bloody face and found a bad cut up near his hairline. "How did you get home?"

"Walked and crawled. I called you but, with the storm and your piano playing, you didn't hear me."

She stared down at him in horror. "Have you been in the shed that long? Oh, I am so sorry!" She filled the dishpan with warm water and washed him off as gently and carefully as she could. She rubbed thick yellow salve on the terrible gashes on his arm and forehead, then bandaged them. "You lost a lot of blood," she said.

"I know," he said weakly.

Laurel pulled off his boots and socks, stood the boots near the washstand to dry and dropped the socks on top of his dirty shirt. "I'll get you dry clothes and be right back. Don't move without my help." She rushed to find clean clothes for him while the storm raged outdoors and the children slept. A fire crackled in the cookstove, warming the kitchen comfortably.

She handed Morgan his clean clothes. "Can you manage alone?"

He nodded weakly.

"I'll go change, too," she said, looking down at her dress which was caked with mud and blood. "Call me if you need help."

"I'll be fine," he said weakly.

She went to her room and changed, then pulled back the covers on the bed. She would convince Morgan to sleep the rest of the day to regain his strength.

A few minutes later she walked into the kitchen to find Morgan in dry blue denims, sitting at the table with his chin in his hand. Muscles rippled across his bare shoulders and back. He lifted his head and looked at her strangely. She flipped her hair over her shoulder and saw him look at it. He had never seen her with her hair down before.

"Who are you, Laurel?"

She frowned. "What do you mean?"

"Are you the woman who is determined to ruin her life over a married man, or are you the woman who tends my kids and me?"

She flushed painfully. "I thought we were going to forget about Fred Saunders."

"And can you do that?"

She moistened her lips with the tip of her tongue. Burning wood snapped. Rain lashed at the windows. "I am trying."

He sighed heavily. "I think you are. But is it possible to forget love and go on from there?"

She stood behind her chair, her breathing shallow. "You mean Rachel?"

He nodded, pain in his eyes. He sat back against the chair. "I think she'll be here waiting for me when I come in from working outdoors. But she never is."

"No. I am."

"Yes. You are."

An icy band squeezed her heart. "I know I'm a disappointment to you, Morgan." She gripped the back of her chair for support. "I will never be Rachel. And I wouldn't want to be her. I am me." She touched her breast. "I am me. Me! Maybe one of these days you'll learn to care for me." Heat rushed over her. Had she really said that to him? How bold and daring!

His dark eyes narrowed. "As you'll learn to care for me," he said with an edge to his voice.

She leaned toward him. "Please, please forget about Fred!"

"I can, but can you?" He moved and winced.

"Enough talk!" She walked to his side and touched his arm. "You are going to lie down and rest on the bed."

"No! Just help me to my rocker."

"No!" She helped him stand. "You are going to do as I say." She took on her teacher's voice and manner. "You will sleep the rest of the day in your comfortable bed. I will take care of everything." She felt him stiffen, but he allowed her to take him to the bedroom and help him into bed.

He sank onto the pillow and closed his eyes. She pulled the cover up to his shoulders. She could smell his damp hair and the special smell of his skin and it left her suddenly weak in the legs.

"I usually sleep on the other side," he said.

"Yes, well, this side will have to do, won't it?" She walked away and pulled the door almost closed behind her. Her legs gave way and she dropped down in his rocker, trembling. "Heavenly Father, help us," she whispered brokenly. "We can't go on like this."

Several minutes later she peeked in and he was sound asleep, snoring softly. She watched him for a while and a warm glow spread through her. She smiled and backed away, pulling the door closed with a quiet click.

When the children awoke she read to them in the kitchen in the soft glow of the lamp. The rain stopped just as it was time to do the evening chores. "Kids, keep very quiet so your pa will sleep. If he does wake up and call for me, take him a drink of water, but tell him I said to stay in bed." She bent down to Worth. "You stay in the kitchen and keep as quiet as a mouse."

"I will keep him quiet," said Hadley, squaring his shoulders.

"I will!" said Diana, frowning at Hadley. "It's my turn!"

Worth leaned his head on the table and just looked at them.

Laurel gathered the eggs, watered and fed the chickens, then walked to the barn to milk Bessie. The barn felt warm and dry and she heard Bessie mooing just outside the barn door. The kitten sat near the milkstool, waiting for warm milk.

Laurel let Bessie into the barn just as Fly, the gelding that had bucked Morgan off, trotted up to the corral. She walked toward the big sorrel, her hand out. "Easy, fella. Easy, Fly. I'll unsaddle you and turn you in to the corral for a drink of water." She reached for the bridle. Fly spun and galloped across the yard, the stirrups flopping wildly.

"You stay out of my garden!" Laurel shouted. Fly stopped near the chicken coop and chomped a clump of grass. With a sigh Laurel walked inside the barn and picked up a bucket. She poured in a little grain and walked outdoors and shook the bucket. "Look, Fly. Come and get it."

Fly lifted his great head, hesitated, then trotted to her. Before he could put his soft black muzzle into the bucket she backed into the barn and he followed. She backed into a stall and poured the grain into a manger. Fly eyed her warily then ducked his head to eat. She unsaddled him, swung the saddle in place and hung the bridle on the wall where Morgan kept it. "There," she said, dusting off her hands and smiling.

Laurel milked Bessie, poured a little warm milk in a bowl for Kitty and walked back to the house. The sun peeked from behind a cloud just in time to set behind the hills in the west.

She stepped inside the kitchen and stopped short. Morgan sat at the table telling the children about his adventure. He looked up and winked at her and kept on talking. The wink zoomed to her heart and did funny things to her that she didn't understand. Her hands trembled as she strained the milk and put it to cool.

When she set supper on the table and after they prayed Morgan said, "We've been trying to decide what to do to celebrate Independence Day next week."

"I think we should have a picnic by the lake and go swimming," said Laurel as she fixed Worth's plate.

"Yes, let's do!" cried Diana. She loved water.

"We could fish," said Hadley who liked to fish, but could go only if Morgan was with him. They hadn't gone once since Laurel came.

"We'll do it," said Morgan, smiling at each one. "We'll have a picnic at the lake and go fishing and swimming. "Laurel, can you swim?"

She nodded. "I learned when I was about Diana's age."

"So did I. The children don't know how. Hadley learned the dog paddle last summer."

"I can swim," said Worth, waving his arms wildly. "I can swim clear across the lake."

"No, you can't," said Diana.

Laurel shook her finger at Worth. "And don't you dare try to swim across the lake by yourself!"

Worth hung his head. "Yes, Ma."

Morgan looked sharply at Laurel just the way he did each time they called her Ma. She ignored his reaction just as she always did.

"I'll fry chicken and make all kinds of good things to take on a picnic," Laurel said, smiling right into Morgan's eyes.

He looked down and spread butter on a slice of bread. Finally he said, "We'll go right after morning chores and spend the whole day. How does that sound?"

"Yippee!" shouted Hadley.

"Let's go now," cried Diana, clapping her hands. Her blue eyes sparkled and her braids flipped around as she bounced on the bench. She turned to Laurel. "Can I help you bake a cake for the picnic, Ma?"

Abruptly Morgan pushed back his chair and walked to the front room.

Laurel turned back to Diana and forced a smile. "You can help me bake a cake. You can all help get ready for the picnic."

She heard Morgan's rocking chair creak and she bent her head to hide her frown.

CHAPTER 8

Independence Day Laurel rode on the high wagon seat beside Morgan as he headed the team toward the lake. She knew his wounds were healing properly and today hadn't needed to be dressed. The past few nights she'd slept on the mat in the front room and insisted that he take the bed. She smiled as she remembered how she forced him to sleep in the bed. When it was time for bed she had curled up on the mat and because he was too weak to carry her away, he'd finally given in. From the corner of her eye she looked at him to see his mood. He seemed happy and she smiled.

The wagon creaked and a hawk cried in the sky. Laurel shielded her eyes against the sun, shining brightly even though it was still early in the morning. She glanced back at the children as they talked and laughed about what they'd do for the special day and repeated what she'd told them about the great United States being free from England's rule for almost a hundred years now. The smell of fried chicken and fresh bread drifted out of the woven clothes basket covered with a heavy white sheet.

"You're quiet, Laurel," said Morgan, resting his arms on his legs with the reins dangling loosely through his gloved fingers. The team walked at an easy pace over the long stretch of prairie grasses, making it possible to carry on a conversation without shouting.

"I'm just enjoying the vacation."

"You are a hard worker, Laurel. I'm thankful for that."

She shrugged, but appreciated his kind words. "Thank you," she said, trying not to sound as surprised as she felt.

"You're a kind, thoughtful woman."

She wrinkled her nose. "Not everybody would agree with that." She cleared her throat. "Morgan, I think it's time we talked about going back to church, don't you?"

He narrowed his eyes thoughtfully. "I don't know, Laurel."

"I know we agreed to wait until we were both ready to be out in public as a family, and I know that I'm the reason you've been putting it off, but I think it's time."

Morgan was quiet for a while and finally nodded. "You're right. I've been thinking the same thing. How about Sunday?" He rubbed his jaw. "Are you ready to face the Saunders family?"

Color stained her cheeks, but she met his gaze evenly. "Yes. Yes, I am. And I won't embarrass either of us."

"I know you won't."

"You do?" That surprised and pleased her. "Have

you really forgiven me?"

He nodded. "I forgave you a while back, but it's taken me a while to act like it. I'm sorry about that."

"I'm sorry about everything," she said around the lump in her throat.

Suddenly Diana squealed and fell against the side of the wagon. "Ma, Hadley pushed me!"

Laurel turned to look back at the children. "What's going on?" she asked sharply.

"I did not push you, Diana!" cried Hadley. "I told you to give me that can of worms."

"He pushed her," said Worth.

Laurel settled the problem, then reached back to feel Worth's forehead. "You're a little flushed, Worth. I want you to sit quietly while we drive so you don't get sick."

"I never get sick," he said, scowling.

Morgan glanced over his shoulder. "Worth, you heard Laurel. You rest."

He settled down and Diana rubbed his head and sang to him.

Laurel smiled and turned around. She saw the horses' ears flick as they walked.

"You sure do know how to keep the kids in hand," said Morgan, grinning.

"My years as a schoolteacher taught me that," she said as she turned to him. His handsome sun-browned face with a slight dimple in his chin, straight nose, high cheekbones and dark brown eyes sent her heart pounding. She forced her voice to stay normal as she said, "You're good with them too."

"That's because they're mine."

She stiffened. "And not mine? Is that what you're saying?"

He frowned. "I didn't mean that."

"Then what did you mean?"

"Drop it, Laurel," he said gruffly, slapping the reins down on the horses to make them pick up their step.

Laurel locked her hands in her lap and rode in painful silence the rest of the way to the lake.

"There it is!" cried Diana.

Laurel had heard a lot about the lake, but this was the first time she'd been there. It covered about three acres of ground and several large cottonwood trees grew along the south side of it with a lone cottonwood on the north side where Morgan stopped the wagon. A sandhill crane standing at the edge of the water flapped its huge wings and flew away with its long legs out behind it. Ducks quacked in alarm and flew up and away in a flutter of wings. Cattle grazed in the distance in the tall grass.

"We're here," said Morgan as he wrapped the reins around the brake handle and jumped to the ground.

Diana, Hadley and Worth pulled off their clothes as Laurel had said they could when they'd dressed this morning, climbed from the wagon and ran toward the water, wearing only their underwear.

"Children, don't go in until I'm with you," Laurel called as she gathered her skirts to climb down over the wheel.

Morgan reached up for her, circled her waist with his large work-hardened hands and lifted her down. Her breath caught in her throat as she stood before him, his hands still on her waist, his eyes boring into hers. He bent his head down until she could feel his breath on her face. For one wild minute she thought he was going to kiss her and her lips tingled with anticipation.

"We're going to have fun today, Mrs. Clements," he said softly.

Happiness exploded inside her and the day suddenly seemed wonderful again. She rested her hands on his broad chest and smiled. She felt the steady thud of his heart and wanted to do something to make it thunder like hers, but she only smiled sedately and said, "Yes, we are, Mr. Clements."

"We'll eat under the tree," he said as he turned away from her and motioned to the huge cottonwood several feet away. Shade spread wide around it and tall grass grew under it.

She carried the blanket to a spot that looked even and spread it out, crushing the grass the best she could. Morgan unhitched the team, watered them and staked them out to graze. Then he set the basket at the edge of the blanket and sat down to pull off his boots and socks. He rolled his pant legs up and she bit back a giggle.

"Did I hear a giggle?" he asked sternly.

She saw the twinkle in his eye and grinned. "I didn't giggle."

"I take it you haven't seen a grown man go wading with his kids."

"Not since my pa went with me."

"Take off your shoes and stockings and let's go take the kids in." He tugged at the hem of her skirt and she laughed and dropped down beside him. She saw a flicker of interest in his eyes before he looked back at the kids and her heart did a strange little flip.

She blushed as she realized Morgan would see her bare feet and ankles. But today she felt very daring. After all, she was his wife!

A few minutes later they ran to the edge of the lake and waded into the sparkling blue water with the kids. "Oh, it's nice and warm," Laurel cried in surprise as she held her skirts high to keep them from getting wet. The sand oozed between her toes and minnows nibbled at her feet. She giggled along with Diana.

"Hold my hand, Worth," said Morgan. "I don't want you walking off on your own."

"I want to swim all the way across," he said, splashing his free hand hard on the water, sending a spray out that hit Diana.

She squealed and waded closer to Laurel. "Stop that, Worth! Make him stop, Pa!"

"You're all right, Diana," said Morgan. "It's all right to get wet. That's what we're here for." He flicked water at Diana and she giggled and buried her face against Laurel's skirt.

"I saw a fish," said Hadley, bending low to peer into the clear water.

"Me too," said Diana. She bent down and looked. Her blond braids dangled down and touched the water. She laughed and bent lower, then even lower until she was sure her braids were wet. Suddenly she tumbled head first into the water.

Laurel grabbed Diana around her waist and lifted her up and out. Diana sputtered and started to cry, but Laurel wiped off her face and laughed. "You wanted to get right down with the fish, didn't you, Diana? I hope you didn't swallow it."

Diana giggled and turned to Morgan. "Pa, Pa, I almost swallowed a fish." She waded to him and caught, his hand telling him in detail her version of what had happened.

He listened to her and laughed, winking over her head at Laurel. The wink seemed to melt her very bones and she almost sank to her knees.

Worth waded to her and sat at her feet, tickling her toes, then giggled. "Did you think I was a fish?" he asked, giggling harder.

Laurel tugged Worth's wet blond hair and laughed. "I thought you were a whole school of fish."

"A school?" Worth frowned up at her.

She nodded and explained to him about fish swimming in schools. He lost interest before she was done and waded to Hadley.

Later Laurel arranged the food on the quilt and called them to come eat. Morgan wrapped a towel around each of them and they ran to Laurel, laughing and shouting. Morgan sat beside Laurel, seeming to fill the space around her and making it hard for her to breathe. He prayed over the food and she managed to compose herself. What would he say if he knew just how he was affecting her?

Worth ate a bite of chicken and two bites of bread. "I want to swim again," he said.

"Later," said Laurel.

"I want to go now," whined Worth.

"Worth," said Morgan in a warning voice and Worth sighed and drooped over his plate.

Diana tugged Laurel's rolled-up sleeve. "Are there bears in those trees, Ma?"

Laurel squeezed Diana's hand reassuringly and shook her head. A couple of days age she'd read them a story about a family in the Colorado Rockies who had a bear walk right up to their cabin. "No bears live in our area, Diana. We're a long way from the Rocky Mountains."

"I heard that there used to be bears here," said Morgan. "But hunters have killed them off or they moved away because there were too many people around."

Before long Laurel found herself discussing Nebraska history with Morgan, especially the ongoing debate about farming the sandy soil that so easily blew away. They talked about raising cattle and horses and crops and the market value of all of it. Morgan said he wondered about the people who were flocking in because of the Homestead Act passed a few years earlier and about the man who had claimed the first one hundred sixty acres.

Laurel listened as she watched the kids running after grasshoppers to see who could catch one first. She told Morgan about her family coming from New York State and how her folks had died, leaving her on her own in Broken Arrow.

He told her about his family coming from Illinois and about marrying Rachel and building the sod house, then later the frame house.

"I'm thankful for a house made of wood with wooden floors instead of dirt," she said.

"I've noticed that you're a very good housekeeper, Laurel."

"Thank you. I try to be." She smiled at him and he smiled at her. For just a minute the world seemed to stand still around them.

"Ma, Ma! Look at Worth!" shouted Diana.

Laurel jumped to her feet, fully expecting to see Worth swimming across the lake. She sighed in relief when she saw him curled in the grass with his eyes closed.

"He's only sleeping," said Morgan.

Diana shook her head. "But I tickled his nose with a weed and he wouldn't wake up," said Diana, sounding close to tears.

Laurel ran to Worth and dropped down beside him. "Worth?" She touched his shoulder and shook him slightly. He didn't open his eyes. She rubbed a hand over his forehead and gasped at the heat she felt. She scooped him up. "Morgan! He's burning up!"

Morgan ran to her and took Worth from her. "Dear God, take care of him," Morgan whispered hoarsely.

Laurel ran to the lake and dipped in a towel, wrung it out and ran back to Morgan. She held the wet towel against Worth and the heat of his body turned the towel hot in her hands.

"Is Worth going to die?" asked Hadley in alarm as he stepped closer to Morgan.

"No!" cried Laurel. "No, he is not."

"We have to get the fever down," said Morgan gruffly as he looked down at him. "He's so tiny. So tiny."

"Why doesn't he move?" asked Diana as tears ran down her cheeks.

Laurel felt Worth's chest rise and fall and she knew he was still alive. She dabbed his body with the towel but it didn't seem to help. "Jesus, take care of our little boy," she whispered. Suddenly she had an idea. "Morgan, take him to the lake and dip him down in the water."

"Yes. Yes, that might work." Morgan half ran, half walked to the lake and out to his knees, then dipped Worth down until only his face was out of the water while Laurel waited at the edge with Diana and Hadley. "He opened his eyes," called Morgan. "Thank you, Lord!"

"I want to swim," said Worth in a weak voice.

Laurel flicked tears off her lashes and laughed.

"Not right now, son," said Morgan with a relieved laugh. "I'm going to hold you in the water a little longer until you're not so hot."

"I got too hot to run after that old grasshopper," said Worth. "I fell down."

"I'm glad he's not dead," said Hadley just above a whisper.

"Me too," said Diana.

"Thank you, Heavenly Father," said Laurel

softly.

A few minutes later Morgan carried Worth to the blanket and Laurel rubbed him dry and dressed him.

"The sun will dry me fast," said Morgan, looking down at his wet blue denims.

"I'm hungry," said Worth, looking around for his plate.

"Then let's get you some food," said Laurel as she handed him the plate that he'd left behind. She had covered it against the flies. "When you're finished, you're going to have a nice nap."

"I want to swim," said Worth.

"You heard your ma," said Morgan.

Laurel's pulse leaped and she hid a smile.

Worth sighed loud and long. "But when I wake up I can swim."

"We'll talk about it then," said Laurel with a laugh.

"I'll take Diana and Hadley for a walk around the lake," said Morgan. "Get your fishing pole, Hadley. We'll be back later."

Laurel watched them walk away as they talked about what they'd see. She turned to Worth and saw that his food was finished. She wiped off his face and hands, then pulled him to her lap, leaned against the trunk of the tree and sang him to sleep.

A few minutes later she laid him on a mat that she'd fixed for him in the back of the wagon and covered him lightly. She brushed back his feather-soft hair and smiled. "Thank You, Father, for this precious boy. Help us to raise him to love You."

She turned at a sound in the distance and saw a horse and buggy approaching. She squinted in the bright afternoon sunlight. Where was Morgan? Did he see the intruder coming toward her? She glanced around but couldn't see Morgan with the children, then turned back to watch the fancy black buggy.

"Nick Stone," she whispered in alarm. What was he doing here? Was he so determined to call this lake his that he'd try to take it by force? She shivered even in the heat.

As the buggy drew closer she saw that Nelda Stone Ross sat beside Nick. She was dressed in black except for a red plume sticking in her hat.

Nick reined in beside Laurel and tipped his hat. He wore a black suit and a crisp white shirt with a string tie that had gold tips. "Well, well," he said. "What are you doing here all alone? Did you run away from the Clements family?"

"My family is here with me," she said coldly. She turned her eyes on Nelda Ross. "Hello, Mrs. Ross."

"Mrs. Clements," said Nelda, tipping her head slightly and making the red plume dance. "I came to see the lake that rightfully belongs to Nick."

"It's a wonderful holiday and I don't want to fight," said Laurel. "You're welcome to climb down and walk around."

Nick's face darkened and his thick mustache twitched. "I don't need an invite to walk around my own lake, Laurel Bennett!"

"Then drive on," she snapped. "This lake belongs to Morgan, as well you know."

"She's right," said Morgan as he stepped around the tree with Diana and Hadley beside him.

Laurel breathed a sigh of relief.

"Where'd you come from?" asked Nick in surprise.

Morgan shrugged. "You are welcome to drive around the lake if you want, Nick."

"The lake is mine!" barked Nick so loud his horse bobbed its head.

Morgan stepped closer. "This is my property, Nick. I have the paper to prove it."

"No paper will change my mind!" With one quick move Nick pulled an ivory-handled Colt from the holster on his hip and pointed the long black barrel right at Morgan's heart.

Laurel bit back a scream as she stared in horror at the Colt, at Morgan, then at Diana and Hadley. They stood perfectly still without speaking, their eyes wide with fear.

"What are you doing, Nick?" cried Nelda, clutching his arm.

He brushed her off and she trembled.

"Don't do it Nick," said Morgan calmly. "You can't kill three children and Laurel too. It's not in you. Not for a piece of property, or not for any reason."

Laurel clutched the sides of her brown gingham dress and bit her lower lip. Would Nick kill them all? She thought of the rifle in the front of the wagon and wondered if she should try to reach it. Pa had taught her to shoot when she was almost too small to hold a rifle. But she knew she couldn't move fast enough to get it.

"Put down the gun, Nick," said Morgan.

Time seemed to stand still as the two men locked eyes in silent combat. A meadowlark warbled nearby, sounding out of place because of the tension.

"Please, Nick," said Nelda. "Don't do this."

Slowly Nick lowered the hammer and slipped the Colt back in the holster. "You're a lucky man, Morgan," he said gruffly.

"God is with me," said Morgan.

Nick slapped the reins on his horse and drove away in a cloud of dust.

Laurel sagged against the wagon, her body drenched with sweat. "Oh, Morgan!"

"Pa!" cried Diana as she buried her face against his leg.

Morgan knelt down and pulled Diana and Hadley close. "I'm all right," he said. "We're all all right." He looked over their heads at Laurel. "I am all right."

"I know," she said weakly.

"Are you?" he asked.

"I don't know." Her hand trembled at her dry throat. She wanted to run to him and have him hold her close, but she couldn't move.

He slowly stood, one hand on each child's shoulder. "Kids, gather up our stuff. Our picnic is over." He watched them run to the blanket, then he slowly walked to Laurel and stopped inches from her, his booted feet apart, his hands resting lightly on his lean hips. "Are you all right?" he asked softly.

She nodded, but whispered, "No, I was so afraid he was going to...to shoot you."

"So was I," he said with a crooked grin.

"You didn't look like it." She trembled and a sob escaped.

He sobered and reached for her. She willingly stepped into his arms and he held her, his cheek pressed against her hair. She clung to him, her eyes closed as his strength flowed into her.

CHAPTER 9

Sunday morning Laurel dried the last plate and piled it on the others in the cupboard. She gripped the dishtowel and sighed. Was she really ready to attend church again? Could she face everyone? She glanced up as Morgan walked in, already dressed in his dark suit and white shirt. He looked so handsome it took her breath away.

"We're leaving soon, Laurel," he said as he reached for his wide-brimmed hat.

She locked her icy fingers together. An ember clinked in the cookstove. The kids talked on the porch just outside the screen door. "Morgan, are you sure you want to go?"

He studied her thoughtfully. "Getting cold feet?"

She looked out the window at the blazing sun, then back at him. "I guess I am." She brushed a strand of glossy brown hair off her flushed cheek. "It'll put quite a strain on you to put on a happy family act, won't it?"

He stiffened. "Are you sure you don't mean it'll be hard on you for Fred Saunders to see you with me?"

She lifted her chin slightly. "I hadn't thought of him. Maybe they won't be there."

"They were always there in the past."

She knew that. She had always sat with them. "You're right, of course."

Morgan worried the wide brim of his hat. "I'll stick close by so you won't be tempted to speak to him."

Sparks flew from her dark eyes. "I won't run away with him."

He was quiet a long time. "I wasn't thinking of that."

"Weren't you?"

"Should I be?"

"No!" She jerked off her apron and balled it up.

"Then I won't let Fred Saunders cross my mind," he said.

She flung the apron to the table. "Just what will you be thinking? That you miss Rachel?"

Pain flashed in his eyes. "Of course I'll miss Rachel!"

"And wish she was here with you instead of me?"

He strode from the house, letting the screen door slam behind him.

She pressed her hands to her flushed cheeks and forced her heart to stop hammering. A great longing rose inside of her and she couldn't move. She heard the kids laugh and a rooster crow.

Finally she walked to her bedroom and chose a blue cotton dress with lace at the collar and cuffs. Tiny blue buttons ran from the high collar, over her full breasts and down to her narrow waist. Her petticoat and skirt fell in graceful folds to her dark shoes. Butterflies fluttered in her stomach. "He can go without me," she whispered in agony. But she knew he wouldn't.

She brushed her thick hair back and up and pinned it carefully so that a few strands curled at her temples. Carefully she set her blue bonnet in place and tied it under her chin. She stood before the looking glass and looked at her large brown eyes, wide mouth and straight nose, then down to her shoes. She pinched her cheeks and moistened her lips with the tip of her tongue. Would anyone guess that she was terrified about facing the church people? She pressed her hand to her stomach to stop the flutters, took a deep breath and walked through the house and outdoors to the waiting wagon. Morgan already had the children seated in the back.

Without a word he helped her up and without a word he slapped the reins and drove away from the yard and out onto the prairie.

To her surprise the children sat in silence all the way to the church. She knew Morgan must have told them to sit quietly.

He pulled up next to another wagon and team. Dust settled as he leaped out and tethered the horses to the hitchrail. Organ music mixed with people greeting each other drifted from the church. The smell of horse manure was strong in the air.

Laurel saw Grove Mayberry standing on the church steps. He called, "Morning, Morgan."

"Morning, Grove," said Morgan in a cheerful

voice.

Without speaking to Laurel, Grove walked into the small white church. She patted her flushed cheeks and tried to steady her racing pulse.

Morgan helped her to the ground and his hands seemed to burn into her waist. He helped the children out and stood by while she retied Diana's belt and bonnet and brushed Hadley's and Worth's hair, then reminded them to take their hats off in church.

She turned in time to see Jane stop short several feet away. Laurel managed to nod and smile slightly. Jane didn't speak or nod, but just stood there, looking years older with dark rings under her eyes and a sallow complexion. Her gray dress hung on her thin frame. Finally she walked to her three daughters and Fred.

Laurel caught his eye, but he looked quickly away without acknowledging her. She flushed and held her drawstring purse to her as she walked with Morgan and the children into the church.

She glanced around to see that most of the straight-backed benches were full. Even with the windows open, the air was heavy and hot. The building looked and smelled and felt very different than when she'd been there for their wedding.

Reluctantly she followed Morgan to an empty bench three rows from the front. He stopped and waited and Laurel started to step in first, but he caught her arm and motioned for Hadley, Diana and Worth to go, then he allowed Laurel to slip in beside Worth and he sat beside her. Her skin burned where he'd touched her and perspiration dotted her face.

His thigh touched hers and he snaked his arm across the back of the seat and curled his hand around her shoulder. "Relax," he whispered with his head close to hers.

She sank against him in relief and let the tension drain away. She really could endure the stares and the whispers with him beside her. She turned her head and smiled and he smiled back.

During the sermon Worth climbed in her lap and fell asleep. Diana and Hadley slid over to take up the empty space and Diana leaned her head against Laurel. Morgan gently lifted Worth off Laurel and held him easily in his strong arms. She peeked at Morgan through her dark lashes and wondered how he truly felt with her beside him instead of Rachel. Would he ever stop thinking about Rachel?

Laurel patted Diana's leg and tried to listen to Pastor Elders, but she couldn't keep her mind on what he said. His voice droned on and on during the closing prayer and she leaned her head against Morgan's arm until he finished.

She glanced up to find Pastor Elders looking right at her and she stiffened.

He cleared his throat and smiled. "We want to welcome Morgan and...Laurel Clements and the children back in our midst. It's good to have you here." He looked around at the congregation. "Greet them and make them feel welcome to our church family. You are dismissed."

"Can we go now?" asked Diana.

Laurel squeezed her hand and nodded. She was as

anxious to get away as the children. Morgan carried
the sleeping Worth down the aisle while Diana and
Hadley squeezed past a heavy-set woman and dashed
outdoors.

Mrs Elders caught Laurel by the arm and stopped
her before she could reach the door. "How've you
been, Laurel?"

"Just fine, Mrs. Elders. And you?"

Mrs. Elders patted her flushed, round cheeks.
"Hot weather never does agree with me, and we
have had some hot days, haven't we?" She leaned
her head closer to Laurel. "Do you know that we
still don't have a teacher? What will we do if we
don't get one?"

"I'm sure they'll find someone," said Laurel,
looking helplessly after Morgan as he walked out
the door.

"But what if they don't, Laurel?"

Laurel shrugged. "I can always teach my own
children."

Mrs. Elders looked at her strangely. "Your
own?"

Laurel gripped her drawstring purse tighter.
"Yes. Hadley, Diana and Worth. Hadley is already
six and Diana will soon be five. They're all quick to
learn and we're very proud of them, Morgan and I
are."

"Yes, well, that's only right, I suppose," said
Mrs. Elders, sounding flustered. "I must speak to
Mabel Proctor if you'll excuse me." She walked
away as she called to Mabel.

Laurel once again started for the door, but bit

back an impatient sigh as she was stopped by Bailey Simms and his oldest daughter. Betsy had finished seventh grade with high marks and would be going into eighth in September. "Hello, Bailey. Betsy, how are you?"

Betsy opened her mouth to speak, but Bailey said, "We're not very well at all, Laurel Bennett."

"Laurel Clements," said Laurel firmly.

He cleared his throat. "Yes. Clements. Of course." He tugged at his stiff white collar. "We need you back to teach, Laurel. Betsy here has cried her eyes out thinking there might not be school this term."

Betsy nodded and her blue eyes filled with large tears.

Laurel patted her arm affectionately, but said to Bailey, "There is still time to find a teacher. Don't give up." She glanced longingly at the door. Was Morgan waiting at the wagon and wondering if she'd gone off with Fred Saunders? "I really must go, Bailey."

"Can't you please come back just to teach until we do find a teacher?" asked Betsy just above a whisper as she twisted the pink strings of her pink and white bonnet. "I have to go to school or I'll never become a teacher like you."

Laurel squeezed Betsy's hand. "You just keep reading and studying on your own, Betsy. You're a good student and you won't fall behind if you do that."

Bailey cleared his throat and his eyes flashed. "You're being stubborn to get back at us, aren't you,

Laurel? You're angry because we forced you into a marriage you didn't want."

Laurel's heart froze in her breast, but she lifted her head high. "Enjoy the rest of the summer, Bailey. Goodbye, Betsy." She pushed past Betsy and excused herself as she nudged hard-of-hearing old Mr. Tredman aside.

Just then someone caught her arm and she turned her head in fear, then smiled at the tall, big-boned woman dressed in a billowing brown and black dress and heavy black bonnet. "Ganny Blake! I am so glad to see you!"

"How've you been, Laurel?" Ganny's voice boomed out and she narrowed her green eyes. "Don't answer that until we're out of ear-shot of all these folks." Ganny easily elbowed her way out the door with Laurel following close behind her.

Ganny led her to a secluded spot at the side of the church near the barn, the parsonage and the out-house. She looked down at Laurel with her hands on her wide hips and her face thoughtful. "Out with it, my girl. What's going on? One minute you're teaching school where I can visit regular with you and the next you're gone from town and married to Morgan Clements." She chuckled. "Not that I wouldn't want to be married to that man if I was twenty years younger. Or even ten!"

Laurel wanted to bare her soul to Ganny, but she knew Morgan wouldn't want that. Had Ganny heard about Fred Saunders? Laurel brushed away a fly and tried to smile brightly. "I wanted a home and a family of my own, Ganny. And he needed a mother for his children."

"I knew his wife had died." Ganny tapped her pursed lips with a long finger. "This is a hard land and a man can't raise a family alone, not when they're as young as Morgan's babies." Ganny nodded. "I reckon I would've done the same thing if I'd been in your shoes."

"I'm not sorry for my decision."

"I'm glad to hear that." Ganny thumped Laurel's chest. "Just what's this I hear about you being kicked out of school over some married man?"

Laurel blushed to the roots of her dark hair. "Ganny, you know I would never take up with a married man!"

"That's just what I told Jane Saunders, but she wouldn't listen to me."

Laurel trembled, suddenly almost too weak to stand. Helplessly she looked around. She heard a cow moo in the barn. Chickens scratched in the corral almost under a mule's hooves. She turned back to Ganny. "I noticed how ill Jane looked today."

"She lost a baby, you know."

A shock passed through Laurel. "When?"

"Maybe three, four weeks ago. She wasn't very far along, but she can't seem to get her strength back. Fred's been anxious about her. Treats her like she's made of glass."

Laurel fingered the strings on her purse. "I hope she gets well soon."

"She's a fine lady, Laurel, and good with her girls and a first-rate cook. But something's been eating at her for a long time now."

Laurel wanted to sink through the sand she stood on.

"I tried to get Jane to open up to me, but she wouldn't. Said she was afraid I wouldn't believe her if she told me. I talked to Fred, but he's like a clam when it comes to telling secrets, especially to a newspaper woman like me."

"I don't know what to say," said Laurel weakly. "I'm sure they can handle their own problems." She managed a smile. "How is the newspaper doing?"

"Not too bad, but if my brother, Harvey, would let me write what I want to write, it'd be a good sight better. Harvey's afraid of the ranchers and the homesteaders. And he is even scared of the shop-keepers. So he doesn't write the news like he should. Makes me plum mad to talk about it!"

"I'm sure it does." She had heard it all before. "Isn't that Harvey talking to Grove Mayberry?"

Ganny nodded. "Who's the other man with them? A stranger. I'll hustle over there and see what's up. Never can tell when I'll run across one of them perfect bachelors who's dying to sweep me off my feet." She slapped her leg and laughed a great bark of a laugh. "It'd take some to do that, now wouldn't it?"

Thankfully Laurel walked back around the building toward the wagon and the people milling around to catch up on all the news. Not many people hurried home after the meeting. Most stayed to talk with people they saw only once a week or less often if they couldn't make it to church each Sunday.

She saw Morgan beside his wagon deep in conversation with a woman Laurel didn't recognize. She saw by the set of his shoulders that he wasn't enjoying the conversation. As she drew closer, she recognized Janice Williams, the town seamstress and wife of the town drunk. Laurel sighed as she hesitated. She didn't want to talk to Janice. Just then Worth ran past and she watched him as he ran off with the other children, playing and shouting and laughing.

With a sigh she walked toward the wagon. She could see that Morgan and Janice didn't notice her. She considered walking away until Janice left but decided she had better rescue Morgan.

"You don't have to put on a happy face for me, Morgan," she heard Janice say. "I know how much you miss your dear, sweet wife. She always loved you so much and so well. She was a quiet little thing, but she had deep feelings. I don't know what she would do if she knew you'd turned so soon to that schoolteacher, Laurel Bennett, what with her bad reputation."

Laurel's jaw tightened and she stepped forward and slipped her hand through Morgan's arm. "Sorry to take so long, Morgan." She smiled at him and she could see by the glazed look in his dark eyes that he desperately wanted to get away. She turned to Janice. "Why, hello, Janice. How are you today? I didn't realize that you knew my husband so well."

"Oh, Laurel," said Janice in a weak voice.

"Morgan, I'll get the children and we can be on our way home." Laurel turned back to Janice. "Or did you have something more to say to my husband?"

Janice pressed her Bible and purse to her. "No. No, we're finished. Have a safe trip...home."

"We will. Thank you." Morgan tipped his head slightly and waited until Janice was out of hearing. "Thank you, Laurel! I was about ready to tell her to get home and take her husband out of his bottle."

Laurel patted his arm. "I'm sorry she gave you such a hard time. Maybe we should have waited a while longer to come to church."

He shook his head. "The worst is over."

"Yes. It is!"

"Pretty rough on you too, huh?"

"Yes." She dabbed perspiration off her forehead and upper lip. "Let's get the kids and go home."

"By next Sunday they'll have something else to talk about and they'll forget about us."

"I hope so." She felt him stiffen and she followed his gaze to see Fred watching them. He stood beside a wagon several feet away. He didn't tip his hat or lift his hand in greeting and Laurel was glad.

"I reckon you talked to him," said Morgan harshly.

"I did not! I said I wouldn't, and I didn't." She tried to pull her hand away from Morgan's arm, but he gripped it in place.

"You disappeared for a while."

"I was with Ganny Blake."

"Am I supposed to believe you?" he asked

harshly.

"Yes!"

Finally he released her hand and she walked toward a group of children playing a game. "Diana. Boys. We're leaving. Boys, get your hats and come on."

The boys ran to where their hats were under a tree. Hadley clamped his in place, then helped Worth find his among the hats of the other boys. Before they could run to the wagon, Jane Saunders marched up to them and grabbed their arms.

Laurel strode forward to make her set them free.

"Is she a good mother to you?" asked Jane in a shrill voice.

The boys tried to pull free, but couldn't.

"I'll handle this," said Morgan as he brushed past Laurel to confront Jane. "Let the boys go, Jane."

Her face crumpled and tears filled her eyes, but she let go of the boys.

They ran to Laurel and she walked them to the wagon and helped them inside along with Diana. Laurel climbed up on the high seat and watched Morgan talking with Jane. What were they saying?

A few minutes later Morgan leaped up on the seat beside her and drove away from Jane and the church and all the people staring after them.

"I don't know if I can do that again," Laurel said weakly.

Morgan didn't answer and she slumped in the seat and watched as they drove out of town and onto the prairie.

"I'm hungry, Ma," said Hadley.

"Me too," said Worth.

Laurel twisted around and flipped a towel off a basket. "I have bread and butter for you. That should keep you until we get home to dinner." She watched them take the bread before she turned to Morgan. "Are you hungry?"

"I'll wait until we're home."

She took a deep breath. "What did she say to you?"

"Nothing worth repeating."

"What was it?"

"Laurel, she's a sick woman. Sick and unhappy."

Laurel ducked her head. "I never, never meant this to happen. I never wanted anyone to know of my secret feelings for Fred." Her voice broke and she moaned.

"It's past and too late now."

"I know. Just tell me what she said."

"Please stop worrying about it. She didn't say anything except that she wanted us to be happy. I told her we are."

Laurel's brows shot up almost to her hairline. "Oh!"

"We are happy. Don't you think?"

"Most of the time."

He nodded and sighed. "I wish you were happy all the time, Laurel, but what's done is done. Fred is not for you."

She frowned. Fred wouldn't make her happy. The startling thought shot through her and she realized that it was true.

In a daze she watched a herd of antelope race across the prairie. She heard Morgan say something to Hadley, but didn't know what he said.

Later as Morgan drove into the yard, he gasped at the sight of a buggy near the porch.

She looked at him to see his face had blanched and his hands trembled. "Who is it?" asked Laurel in alarm.

"Rachel's family," he said so low that she had to strain to hear him.

She pressed her hand to her throat. Rachel's family! How could she deal with Rachel's family?

CHAPTER 10

"Rachel's family?" whispered Laurel as shivers ran up and down her spine. She heard the children asking about the company, but her head spun too much to answer them. She reached out to Morgan for support and realized that he was more upset than she.

He stopped beside the buggy, but just sat there, the reins between his fingers and his arms on his legs.

Laurel looked at the two women and the man who stood near the porch where she'd planted the cactus. The women were both blond and attractive and looked very much alike and very much like Rachel Clements! The man was short and wiry with black hair and snapping black eyes. The women ran toward the buggy, but the man walked at a leisurely pace, his hands in his pockets.

"Morgan!" cried the women. They spoke in the same off-key voice. "Children! How you've grown!"

"Hello," whispered the children together.

"This is a surprise," said Morgan weakly.

"Who is this?" asked the woman nearest to

Morgan as she pointed up at Laurel.

Morgan dropped to the ground, helped the children out, then reached for Laurel. He stood her beside him and kept his arm around her waist.

She felt him tremble and tried to think of something to say that would help him.

"This is my wife," he finally said. "My wife, Laurel."

The women gasped the same gasp and both pressed their hands to their hearts in the same manner. The man hid a grin.

"Your wife?" the women asked in the same shocked voice.

Morgan's arm tightened around Laurel and she knew the situation was very hard on him, but she didn't know what to do to help him. "Laurel, this is Rebecca, Rachel's twin sister and her older sister, Esther." He motioned to the man. "This is Bud Abbott, Esther's husband. They live near Omaha."

Rebecca eyed Laurel as if she was a rattlesnake. "I can't believe this, Morgan! You didn't say a word about being married again! You knew we were coming to see you this month! We talked about it at the funeral."

Laurel knew the mention of Rachel's funeral hurt Morgan, so she stepped forward with a smile. "Won't you come inside? It's cooler in there. And I'll make dinner."

"I want to speak to Morgan alone," said Rebecca. "Esther, you and Bud go inside. You kids, go in too."

"I think I should stay to talk with Morgan,

too," said Esther. "Bud, take the kids and go inside with...with Laurel, wasn't it?"

Laurel nodded and started inside, but Morgan caught her arm. "I'm going in with you."

"No!" cried Rebecca with a pout. "We must talk, Morgan, and you know it."

With a sigh he turned back to Rebecca. "You're right. Let's get it over with. I'll be in later, Laurel."

She walked inside and sank to a chair as Bud and the children talked and laughed together while they drank from the bucket of water on the washstand.

"I'll go fill the bucket with fresh water," said Bud, smiling at Laurel. "If that's all right with you."

She nodded, at a loss for words.

Hadley leaned against Laurel and whispered, "They look just like our other ma."

"They do," said Diana.

"I didn't know that," said Worth.

Laurel smiled. "They are your mother's sisters. Diana is your sister, Hadley. And yours, Worth. Rebecca and Esther and your ma were sisters. You saw them before at the funeral."

"I remember," said Hadley.

"I never saw them before," said Diana.

"Me neither," said Worth.

"You just don't remember," said Laurel. She eased off her bonnet and dangled it from her fingers as she talked to them.

Bud brought in the fresh water and set it in place.

He turned around and grinned. "Kids, I hear you have a kitten in the barn. Want to show it to me?"

They ran to him and Laurel smiled thankfully at him. He smiled a knowing smile and nodded slightly.

"We'll be back later," he said.

"Take your time, Bud."

"Don't let the ladies scare you, Laurel," he said over his shoulder as he walked out the door.

Laurel ran to the front room and scooped up Morgan's pallet, carried it to the bedroom and hid it under the bed. She threw open all the windows and let the wind blow in. Even though it was hot wind, it was fresher than the closed-in air of the house. She ran a dustcloth over the furniture and tied a flowered apron around her dress. Starting the fire, she opened jars of canned beef, washed new potatoes from the garden and slid the pot of fresh-snapped green beans onto the stove. Working quickly she soon slid a large pan of biscuits into the oven, then set the table with the china and good glasses. She felt flushed and hurried but she kept working, always listening for steps on the porch. Just what were Rachel's sisters saying to Morgan?

Finally Morgan opened the door and let the women walk in first. They took off their big flowered hats and fanned themselves. He walked to Laurel's side and slipped an arm around her shoulders. She hid her surprise as she smiled at him.

"They're staying the night, Laurel. I told them you wouldn't mind at all." He squeezed her shoulder enough to let her know to go along with him and she manged to smile even wider.

"Dinner will be ready soon. I'm sure you'll want to wash off the dust of the trip before you sit down to eat." Laurel pointed to the clean towel that she'd draped over the rack at the washstand.

"We'll put Bud and Esther in the boys' bed and Rebecca in Diana's," said Morgan. "The kids can sleep on the floor and that way we won't have to give up our bed." He stressed *our,* but she didn't think the women noticed.

Laurel nodded without giving away even by the flicker of an eyelash the shock that ran through her body. He didn't want Rachel's family to know that they didn't share a bed! "It won't be any trouble. I'll put clean bedding on the beds," she said brightly. She felt Morgan relax.

He turned his head enough that the women couldn't see his face and mouthed, "Thank you."

By the time dinner was over and the dishes washed and put away, it was time to do evening chores. Laurel got the milk pail from the pantry, but Morgan took it from her hands.

"Bud, come to the barn with me while I milk," Morgan said.

"Why doesn't Laurel do the milking?" asked Rebecca. "Rachel always did. I would if I lived here."

"Laurel does the milking when I can't, but tonight I can do it. Coming, Bud?"

"Right with you, Clem." Bud walked out the door and stood on the porch long enough to roll a cigarette and light it. The smoke drifted back inside and Laurel frowned. She hated for the children to be around anyone who smoked.

Rebecca paced the floor while Esther sat at the table sipping a cup of coffee.

Suddenly Rebecca stopped in front of Laurel. "I understand that you're a Christian."

"Yes," said Laurel, taken aback.

Rebecca rolled her eyes. "Rachel always felt it was important and she didn't marry until she found a man who was also religious. Esther and I believe in God, of course. Everyone does, I'm sure. But we're not fanatics about it like Rachel was."

Laurel lifted her chin. "I wouldn't call myself religious, nor did Rachel. She had a personal relationship with God. So do I and so does Morgan. We're raising the children to have a great love and trust in God."

Rebecca waved the words away. "It doesn't make sense to me. But as I told Morgan, I have no objections."

"Oh, really?" Laurel couldn't see why it mattered one way or the other to Rebecca. It wasn't any of her business.

Several minutes later Morgan brought in the milk and eggs and she took them gratefully while he was forced to visit with his company.

Laurel served a light supper, then put the children to bed in the front room on the floor. She moved the rocker out of the way and carried it into the bedroom. Her stomach fluttered. Soon she would share the room with Morgan. Could she do it? She had no choice. She took a deep breath and silently prayed for help.

In the kitchen she sat at the table and listened as the others talked about people she didn't know and times she'd never shared in. She was glad when they called it a night and went to bed.

"I'll go check on the animals and be right in," said Morgan as he walked to the door.

She nodded. He was as nervous as she. She carried the lamp to the bedroom and set it on the dresser, then quickly changed into her nightdress and slipped on her robe. Butterflies fluttered in her stomach and her body burned, then pricked with icy chills. She sat in the rocker gripping the smooth arms of it as she listened for Morgan's footsteps.

Finally the door opened and he stepped inside. He jabbed his fingers through his hair and sighed as he looked at Laurel. "What a long day," he said tiredly.

"Yes," she said.

He walked with easy grace across the room and looked down at her. "They were really surprised about us. I know I should have written, but I just couldn't bring myself to do it." He sank down on the trunk beside the rocker. Shadows danced on the wall. Night sounds drifted through the open window along with a plesantly cool breeze. "I just couldn't write."

She pleated her wrapper over her legs. "I think they came for a special reason."

He groaned and rubbed his hand over his face. His whiskers sounded raspy. "They did."

"What was it?"

"Rebecca expected to stay."

Laurel leaned forward with a gasp. "To stay?"

"And marry me."

Laurel shot up and the rocker banged against the wall. "What?"

Morgan slowly stood and she stepped up so close to him she could smell his skin and feel his breath on her face. "You mean you didn't have to marry me?" she hissed. "You could've had Rebecca to help with the kids?"

He gripped her arms and whispered, "I knew that she planned to take over where Rachel left off and I knew I couldn't stand her to!"

"But why me?"

"You were what I needed."

"Oh." She didn't know if she should be pleased or angry.

He loosened his grip, but kept his hands curled around her arms. "Rebecca is self-centered and not fit to mother our kids."

"But she's Rachel's sister!"

"I know. Rachel was one of a kind. She looked like her sisters, but never acted like them. Jesus made the difference."

Laurel studied Morgan in the dim light from the lamp. "Maybe she wanted Rebecca here in her place."

"I already told you that she chose you."

Laurel trembled. "But she was wrong about me."

He rubbed his hands up and down her arms. "No, she wasn't." His voice was so low she had to strain to hear. The words were like beautiful music to her ears.

She lifted her hands and rested them lightly on his chest. She felt the thud of his heart and the warmth of his skin through his shirt. "What about Fred?"

"You made a mistake. We've all made mistakes."

"Yes. Yes, we have."

"But you corrected yours."

She groaned. "But not before I hurt that family."

"I know." He gently pushed her curtain of rich brown hair back from her face and over her shoulders. "They'll get over it with God's help."

"I know." She wanted to ask him if the raw pain of losing Rachel had passed yet, but she couldn't force the words out and break the bond she felt between them.

"You were wonderful today, Laurel. Thanks for not giving me away to them."

"I would never do that to you."

He ran a finger down her cheek, leaving a trail of fire. "You are quite a woman. You could've panicked when you realized that we would share a room tonight, but you didn't."

She laughed softly. "I did panic, but I just didn't let it show." She didn't want to move away from him, but she stepped back and managed to keep her voice normal. "Just how will we work it for tonight?"

He was silent for so long that her nerves tightened until she thought they'd snap. Finally he shrugged. "I'll sleep on the floor. And try not to snore." He laughed, but it was a shaky laugh and she knew he was as affected by her as she was by him.

She'd used his mat for the kids, so she pulled two quilts out of her trunk and spread them on the floor, than handed him his pillow. His hand brushed hers and sparks flew. She couldn't move away or speak.

He stood with the pillow against his chest. "Laurel, I'm not sorry that I married you instead of Rebecca."

"You're not?" she whispered.

"No." A lock of dark hair fell across his wide forehead and she wanted to reach up and brush it back, but she locked her hands behind her back.

"I'm not sorry either," she said softly.

"We'd better get to sleep," he said, but he didn't move.

"It has been a long day." She slowly turned and cupped her trembling hand around the globe and blew out the lamp. She draped her robe over the end of the bed and slipped between the sheets. She heard Morgan settle down on the quilts and his presence seemed to fill the room.

Just then the moon broke from behind a cloud and lit a path from the window to the bed. A cricket chirruped. An owl hooted. Laurel lay very still, her eyes wide open. "Morgan," she whispered.

"Yes?"

She bit her bottom lip. "I'm glad I didn't run off with Fred."

"So am I."

"I'm glad I married you."

"You are?" He sounded pleased and she smiled.

"I am." She turned on her side. "Good night, Morgan."

"Good night, Laurel."

"Sleep tight."

"You too."

She listened to him breathe and finally heard him fall asleep. She snuggled into her pillow and closed her eyes.

The next morning she opened her eyes to find him gone. The sun peeked up over the horizon and bathed the room in warm light. Morgan's neatly folded quilts hung over the foot of the bed and his pillow was in place next to hers. She touched it and her face flamed. How would it feel to wake up each morning with him beside her?

With a gasp she swung out of bed and dressed quickly.

She glanced in the looking glass and caught sight of her tangled hair and sparkling eyes and pink cheeks.

"He saw me sleeping!" she whispered, turning as red as one of the quilt squares.

She grabbed up her brush and brushed her hair with quick, impatient strokes, then pulled it back and pinned it in place.

Could she face him this morning as if nothing had changed between them? She frowned. Nothing *had* changed.

She tip-toed through the front room where the children still slept soundly. In the kitchen she found a pail of warm, foamy milk to strain and a fire already burning in the cookstove. Just how long had Morgan been up?

She stepped out on the porch and breathed deeply of the pleasantly cool morning air. A rooster crowed while hens scratched in the dirt. She looked around for Morgan, but he wasn't in sight. Disappointed, she walked back inside, fixed the fire and strained the milk. She poured yesterday's cream into the churn, then quickly made coffee and mixed up a batch of pancakes.

Hadley walked in with Diana and Worth trailing behind. They were dressed in the clothes Laurel had laid out for them.

"A cricket tried to eat my ear last night," said Worth, frowning.

"It did not," said Diana.

"It was in the fireplace and it was only making a noise," said Hadley. He yawned widely. "I tried to get it, but I couldn't."

Laurel hugged and kissed them. "Fill the woodbox and see if your pa watered the chickens. Breakfast should be ready when you finish."

They ran out and she poured batter onto the hot griddle. The smell from the pancakes and coffee made her stomach growl. When the pancakes were done, she broke a dozen eggs into the big cast iron skillet to fry.

The screen door squeaked and she turned her head to see Morgan walk in. He pulled off his wide-brimmed hat and smiled at her.

"Anything for a hungry man to eat?"

She smiled and couldn't take her eyes off him. "I

think we could find something," she said breathlessly.

"The kids will be right in with wood."

"Good."

"Are the others up?" he nodded toward the front room.

"Not a peep."

"I'll fix that." He strode to the bedroom door and she heard him knock loudly and say, "Breakfast is ready and waiting. Come and get it now or you go without." He walked back to the kitchen, chuckling. "That should get them going."

Laurel set the plate of eggs on the table near the pancakes. "Are they leaving this morning?"

"I think they will." He grinned at Laurel and bobbed his dark brows. "But it's up to us to see that they do."

She giggled. "What'd you have in mind?"

He leaned down close to her and whispered, "We have to convince them that we're happily married."

"But they know that you're not over Rachel yet."

He shrugged. "I want Rebecca to know that I am married to you now and plan to stay married to you."

"You could just tell her that."

"I tried, but she still thinks I'm going to get tired of you and want her because she's *family*."

"And will you get tired of me?" whispered Laurel.

"What a crazy question! Will you help me, or not?"

She nodded. "I'll do what I can."

"Thank you." He tapped the tip of her nose with his finger and grinned. "You won't regret it. We don't want her here, making life miserable for all of us, the kids, especially. She has this crazy notion that she's going to stay on while Esther and Bud go back home."

"We'll see about that!" snapped Laurel in her best schoolteacher voice.

Morgan laughed and patted her back. "That's my girl."

Her heart leaped so hard she was sure he'd notice.

The kids walked in and dumped their wood into the woodbox with a loud thud and she was able to force her pulse back to normal.

"Wash and eat, kids," Laurel said brightly. As she turned to help Worth, the company walked into the kitchen, dressed and looking wide awake. Laurel wondered if they'd been up long before Morgan called them, talking quietly and making plans of their own. She set her jaw stubbornly. Nothing they could plan would make a difference!

"Smells good in here," said Bud, smiling as he breathed in the coffee aroma.

"I am hungry," said Esther as she washed her hands, then sat on the bench with Bud on one side of her and Diana on the other.

Rebecca sat on the bench with Worth and Hadley. After Morgan said the blessing on the food, she fixed Worth's plate and even tried to feed him. "Open wide," said Rebecca.

He scowled at her and took the fork from her.

Laurel hid a smile behind her coffee cup.

"He is three years old, Rebecca," said Morgan. "He's been feeding himself for a long time."

"I guess I forget how big he is." she said, smiling at Worth and wrinkling her nose. "You're such a precious, pretty little thing."

Laurel knew Worth wouldn't take being called pretty, so she said quickly, "Bud, have many new homesteaders settled in your area since spring?"

"Sure have. But I can tell most of 'em won't stay. It takes a lot to prove up a homestead and make it into a home."

Morgan kept Bud talking most of breakfast.

Later Laurel excused the children from the table and refilled the coffee cups for the others. She sat quietly, sipping another cup of coffee while the women talked to Morgan. Esther really was quite nice, but Rebecca seemed spoiled and selfish. As Rebecca talked on and on Laurel forced herself to sit quietly. She had butter to churn, mending and sewing to do and lessons to teach the children. She knew Morgan had a horse to finish breaking for a neighbor as well as a fence to check.

Finally Rebecca stood and flipped her blond curls over her shoulders. "Morgan, may I speak to you privately outdoors?"

"Sure," he said with a smile, pushing back his chair. "We'll take a walk outdoors."

Laurel stiffened. Why was Morgan suddenly happy about talking alone with Rebecca? A twinge of jealousy shot through Laurel. Abruptly she stood up and reached for the plates to stack them.

At the door Morgan turned and smiled at Laurel. "Coming?"

She brushed her hands down her apron and nodded. So, he knew exactly what he was doing! "Certainly," she said as she walked to his side and slipped her arm through his. Rebecca frowned. "But Morgan, I want to speak to you alone."

"You can't say anything that I wouldn't want my wife to hear," he said as he led the way off the porch.

Rebecca stopped after a few steps and stamped her foot. "I will not take another step until you tell me why you won't give me a few minutes of your time."

Laurel looked up at Morgan and smiled. "I'm sure I can spare you a minute. But that's all." She turned to Rebecca and sighed heavily. "I really can't part with him for very long without missing him so much."

Rebecca scowled. "That's ridiculous!"

Laurel shrugged. "I don't think so." She squeezed Morgan's arm. "I'm glad you married me when you did. I couldn't have lived a day longer without you." She playfully shook her finger at Rebecca and laughed. "Don't you try to convince him to divorce me and marry you. I wouldn't let that happen. He's mine now and I'm going to hang on tight to him!"

"And I'm going to hang on tight to you," said Morgan with a chuckle as he hugged Laurel. "You're the only woman for me."

Rebecca's face turned bright red. "What a ter-

rible display of affection right in front of everyone!" She whirled around, lifted her skirts off the
dusty ground and marched back to the house, calling, "Esther! Bud! I'm ready to go home."

Laurel bit back a giggle and looked up at Morgan
as the screen door slammed behind Rebecca. He
shook with silent laughter.

"Good work," he whispered.

"Thanks." She walked to the house with him,
his arm around her shoulders and her arm around his
waist. She stopped at the screen door and their eyes
locked. Time seemed to stand still. The sounds of
the children playing in the yard seemed to come
from a great distance. A sharp word from Rebecca
brought Laurel back to reality. Flustered, she
dropped her arm, eased away from Morgan and
reached for the door handle.

CHAPTER 11

Laurel ran to the cold kitchen to catch Morgan before he disappeared for the day. Last night she'd decided that no matter how early she had to get up, she'd catch him and make him talk to her. She had let his silence continue much too long. She stopped just inside the kitchen and sighed in disappointment. He was gone already. "Maybe he's still at the barn," she muttered as she slipped on Morgan's old jacket and grabbed the milk pail and egg basket.

She ran across the frost-covered yard, the weak sun barely peeking above the horizon in the east. Suddenly she stopped. Fly was gone from the corral. "Morgan's gone again," she said with a sob catching in her throat.

Weakly she sank to the cold bench near the pump. Was he really trying to avoid her? Or was he as busy as he seemed?

She watched Kitty come from the barn and meow as if to ask where the morning milk was. Laurel searched the vast countryside for a sign of Morgan, but this morning nothing moved that she could see except a hawk in the sky. She shivered as October wind blew her skirts against her ankles. She rubbed her hand across her nose. Since Rachel's family had visited, Morgan had withdrawn worse than when she first came last spring.

But why?

She picked at a loose thread on her dress as her lip quivered. Did he think she wanted more than he could give? They had been so close the night they shared the bedroom!

She had tried to talk with him since then, but he left early and came home late each night. Then he was too tired to do more than eat and drop onto his mat near the fireplace. As the days passed from hot summer to the cool days of fall, she tried to find an answer. Morgan kept her at arm's length all of the time, even when they went to church. He was always polite but he never touched her except to help her in and out of the wagon.

"He *is* avoiding me," she whispered as a tear slipped down her cheek. What could she do?

"I'll talk to him! Somehow!" she said firmly as she marched to the chicken coop to let out the chickens, then strode to the barn to milk the cow. The barn was warm and smelled of hay.

Kitty mewed and rubbed against Laurel's leg. She milked Bessie as fast as she could, and walked to the house to start the fire and strain the milk.

After a breakfast of pancakes, sausage from the pig that Morgan had butchered two weeks ago, eggs and milk she told the children to dress warm for outdoors. "We have to carry the squash and pumpkins to the cellar," she said as she stacked the dishes to wash later. They had already spent days digging potatoes and carrying them to the cellar. She had canned the tomatoes, green beans, and carrots.

Diana and Hadley ran to get their coats while Worth stayed at the table. Laurel touched his forehead but it was cool and normal. Twice in the past two months he'd had a high fever.

"What's wrong, Worth?" she asked. "You're always first out the door."

"I want school," he said.

She kissed the top of his blond head. "Later, Worth." The school board had not found a teacher so she taught Hadley at home. Diana and Worth joined right in. Worth could already say all the letters of the alphabet and quote several Scriptures. "Get your coat on. Be sure to put your warm hat on. It's really cold out."

"Will it snow?" asked Diana.

"It might," said Laurel as she dressed in Morgan's coat and wrapped a thick scarf around her head and neck. "Frost hit twice already. We must get the squash and pumpkins in before it snows."

By noon they had one more load to carry to the cellar. Laurel stood at the edge of the garden. Cold wind blew against her, chilling her to the bone. The boys had red cheeks and noses. She glanced around with a frown. "Boys, where's Diana?"

"I don't know," said Worth as he struggled with a big pumpkin.

"Maybe she went to the toilet," said Hadley.

"Maybe," said Laurel. She filled Hadley's cart with the last squash and sent them to the house. "You boys take these inside. And wipe your nose,

Worth!"

She looked toward the outhouse. Just how long had Diana been gone? An uneasy feeling grew inside Laurel and she shouted, "Diana! Where are you?"

She expected to hear a shout from the outhouse, but none came and she frowned. She cupped her cold hands around her mouth. "Diana!" Sometimes Diana went inside the chicken house to talk to the chickens. Laurel called again, then again.

"I'll check the barn," said Hadley, coming back from unloading the cart. He ran across the yard.

"Thanks, Hadley." Laurel scanned the prairie for a little girl in a blue bonnet and coat. She saw waving dried grass, cattle, plowed fields and a few birds flying across the vast, gray, threatening sky.

Worth slipped his cold hand into hers. "Is Diana lost?"

"I hope not. I can't imagine her just disappearing."

"She probably went to see the bull," said Worth, his blue eyes wide and innocent.

Laurel's stomach tightened. "Why would she go there? She knows she's not supposed to go near the bull."

Worth shrugged until his head was almost lost between his shoulders.

"Worth?" Laurel's voice was firm as she frowned down at him.

"She likes to tease him and see him snort and paw the ground. But I don't!" he said quickly. "Just Diana does."

A chill trickled down Laurel's spine. She knew

just by looking at and listening to Worth that both he and Diana had gone to see the bull even though they weren't supposed to. "And when have you two gone to tease the bull?"

Worth ducked his head and twisted his boot in the dirt. "Tuesdays we do."

Laurel had been teaching them the days of the week and Worth could only remember Tuesday. Any day of the week was Tuesday to him. "Did you tease the bull yesterday while I worked in the cellar?"

"Was yesterday Tuesday?"

"Worth!"

He looked up at her and finally nodded. "But we didn't climb over the fence. We didn't get any closer than the fence."

"Oh, my!" Laurel lifted her skirts and ran toward the bull's corral. Morgan had built an extra sturdy fence and gate and had warned the children never to go near it. She thought they had obeyed after the time she caught them there.

She thought of the danger and pictured Diana in a crumpled heap at the bull's feet or even a bloody pulp under the bull's hooves. "Keep her safe, Lord," she said as she ran.

She slid to a stop at the fence and peered over the top board. The huge bull stood at the far side of the corral near a tall cottonwood. Diana was not in sight. Laurel sagged against the fence in relief. Worth and Hadley ran up and stood beside her.

"Where is she?" asked Hadley fearfully.

"Is she squashed?" asked Worth, trembling as he

peered through the two middle boards.

"She's not here," said Laurel.

Just then she heard a tiny frightened voice calling, "Ma! Help! Ma!"

Blood pounded in Laurel's ears and a bitter taste filled her mouth. She gripped the top rail of the fence and forced back the panic that threatened to swamp her as she looked for Diana.

"Look!" cried Hadley, pointing at the first tree in the clump.

"Look at Diana!" shouted Worth, jumping up and down.

Laurel finally spotted Diana clinging to a small branch and standing on another just inches from the bull's massive head.

"Ma!" cried Diana.

The bull bellowed and shook its great head.

"Where's Pa?" asked Hadley, shivering.

"Pa will spank her hard," said Worth.

"She needs to be spanked," snapped Laurel. She walked along the fence, her body weak and trembling. How she needed Morgan to ride in and save Diana! But she didn't dare wait for Morgan. "Help me, Lord," she prayed. "Thank you for wisdom and courage!"

Suddenly she spun around and faced the boys. "I'll need your help, boys."

"What do you want us to do?" asked Hadley.

"I'll punch that bull right between the eyes," cried Worth, jabbing the air with his tiny fists.

"I have to get to Diana but I can't with the bull standing under the tree she's in." Laurel took a deep breath. "You boys climb through the fence and shout at the bull and wave your hats. When the bull runs toward you, you slip under the fence to safety and I'll run to Diana." Laurel bent down to the boys. "Can you do it?"

"Yes," said Hadley calmly.

"Yes," said Worth with a grin.

"You'll have to make sure the bull is looking at you while I'm inside the corral. Don't let him look at me." She hugged them both. "I'll run down the fence a ways. Once the bull is looking at you, I'll run to Diana." Laurel forced back a shiver as she ran down the fence line. Suddenly Morgan's coat felt too hot. Her scarf scratched her cheeks and neck and she tugged on it. She turned toward the boys and called, "I'm ready, boys."

They slid under the bottom rail and ran a short way into the corral. Hadley pulled off his hat and waved and shouted. Worth flapped his arms and shouted. The bull turned his massive head and bellowed, but didn't move. The boys yelled louder. Worth danced a little jig, but the bull ignored him. Hadley dashed toward the bull, then back to the fence, but the bull didn't move.

Laurel waited, every nerve tense. Finally she pulled her scarf off and called to Hadley. "Come to the fence!" She ran along the fence and pushed the scarf into his hands. "Wave this. Wave it hard! But wait until I'm back in place." She ran to her spot and shouted that she was ready. Icy wind whipped her skirts around her cold legs. She glanced up at the sky to see dark snow clouds rolling in.

Hadley waved the scarf and yelled. Worth pulled off his coat and waved it and shouted at the bull. Finally the bull turned to face the boys. It snorted and pawed the ground, sending dirt flying. With its head down it galloped across the corral, its hooves pounding the ground. Laurel slipped through the fence, lifted her skirts high and ran toward the tree that held Diana. Laurel wanted to see if the boys were safe, but she didn't dare turn to look. She heard them continue to yell at the bull.

Diana cried out and Laurel reached up and lifted her to the ground. Tears streamed down Diana's ashen face and she clung to Laurel with a death grip. Laurel turned to see the bull over near the fence, pawing the ground and snorting at the boys who were safely on the other side.

"Hang on tight, Diana," Laurel said grimly as she held Diana to her. She knew she couldn't run as fast carrying Diana. She took a deep breath and raced across the corral. Her mouth felt bone dry and a pain stabbed her side. She reached the fence and pushed Diana through, then glanced over her shoulder to see the bull almost on top of her.

"Ma!" screamed the boys, running toward where Diana stood.

Laurel's legs almost buckled under her, but she leaped up on the fence and scrambled over just as the bull thundered past. She fell in a heap on the ground and gasped for breath. The children huddled around her, their faces white. Finally she pushed herself up, took the scarf from Hadley and wrapped it around her head and neck.

"Let's go to the house, kids. We have school."

"Look! Here comes Pa!" cried Worth, pointing as Morgan rode toward them on Fly.

"Don't tell him that I went in the corral," said Diana.

Laurel watched Morgan sitting high in the saddle as he rode nearer. She bent down to Diana. "We will tell Pa and you will get spanked. You can not disobey."

"I know," whispered Diana as she slipped a small, cold hand into Laurel's.

Laurel gripped the tiny hand and walked purposefully toward Morgan. He swung out of the saddle and left the reins dangling to the ground. He looked cold and tired. His sheepskin-lined jacket collar was turned up to protect his neck. Chickens squawked and ran out of his way. The boys stayed close beside Laurel and Diana.

"What's wrong?" Morgan asked when they reached him.

Worth started to speak, but Laurel stopped him.

"Diana," Laurel said, "Tell your pa."

Diana's lip trembled and she hung her head.

"Diana," said Laurel sternly.

Finally Diana looked up at Morgan. "I climbed in the bull's corral and got stuck in a tree."

"What?" cried Morgan in alarm.

"She was teasing the bull," said Worth.

Morgan slapped his hand hard against his leg. "What has been going on here, Laurel? I thought you could take care of the kids. But it seems like I was wrong."

Laurel stared at him in shock. He was blaming her!

"Did you spank her?" asked Morgan sharply.

"No," said Laurel.

"Why not?" Morgan rammed his hat on his head. A muscle jumped in his jaw and fire shot from his dark eyes. "What kind of mother are you? How can you let Diana do that without spanking her?"

Tears welled up in Laurel's eyes. She tried to blink them away, but they slipped down her cold cheeks. With a strangled cry she ran toward the barn for privacy, then stopped beside Fly. She scooped up the reins, gathered her skirts and swung into the saddle. The stirrups hung down too far for her feet, but she didn't care. She had to get away from Morgan and the children.

"Come back here, Laurel!" shouted Morgan.

"Ma!" cried the children.

Laurel slapped the reins against Fly and shouted to him. He galloped out onto the prairie and away from the yard and Morgan. Icy wind whipped against Laurel, but she couldn't feel it through her misery.

A pack of coyotes ran from behind a low hill, then out of sight. Fly fairly flew around hills and over low rises. Suddenly cold snow stung Laurel's face. She slowed Fly and turned him toward the trail. She didn't want to get lost in the open prairie, especially with snow flying hard around her.

Gradually she calmed down, then realized that her hands were too cold to hold tightly to the reins. She hunkered down into Morgan's coat. The wind whipped her gray skirts off her legs. She slowed Fly to a walk and rubbed the moisture off her face. The air was filled with large, white flakes of snow that clung to her lashes and clothes and Fly's mane.

"I must turn back," Laurel muttered. She couldn't stay out any longer. Morgan and the children were probably worried about her. It wasn't like her to lose control.

Reluctantly she turned toward home. By the time she reached the barn, it was dark. A fine blanket of snow covered the ground. She knew Morgan would have milked and done the other night chores. She unsaddled Fly, fed and watered him and put him in a stall for the night. Kitty rubbed against her leg and mewed contentedly. Bessie mooed. "I guess I'd better go inside," Laurel whispered.

Light shone from the kitchen window and she moaned. Could she face Morgan after running away? She brushed snow off her face as she slowly walked toward the house.

Maybe Morgan would tell her to pack her things and leave. She stopped with a low whimper. He might not ever want to see her again. Or he might stop talking to her at all. "It can't really get any worse," she muttered, her lips almost too cold to move.

She walked onto the porch, hesitated at the door, then opened it. Smells of coffee and fried pork chops drifted out. She stepped inside and the warmth wrapped around her.

Morgan turned from the stove, his look guarded.

"Laurel," he said with a slight nod.

She hooked her tangled hair over her ears. "Hi," she whispered.

"Are you hungry?"

"A little, maybe." She slipped off the coat and hung it on the hook beside the door next to Morgan's heavy coat.

"I saved a plate of food for you," he said as he opened the warming oven and pulled out the plate. He set it on the table along with a cup of coffee.

Her hands tingled as she washed them in the warm water. She brushed her hair and sat at the table. The potatoes, pork chop, string beans and biscuit made her stomach growl. She glanced at Morgan as he stood with his back to the stove, his thumbs looped over his belt. "Aren't you going to have something?"

He shrugged. "Coffee, I reckon." He poured himself a steaming cup and sat on the bench in Diana's place beside Laurel.

Having him so close made her stomach tighten. She picked up her fork, but couldn't force herself to take a bite.

"I was afraid you weren't coming back," he said softly.

"I had to get away." She laid the fork down and locked her hands in her lap, staring at her food.

"The kids told me what happened. I'm sorry for getting mad at you."

Finally she looked at him. "I knew you'd be sorry."

He fingered his cup. "I am."

"But it doesn't make me feel any better."

He sighed. "I know." He reached for her hand and she let him take it and hold it. "Your hand's cold."

"I know." The warmth of his hand reached to her heart and she smiled. "It's cold out."

"Laurel, please forgive me. You're a wonderful mother to the kids. I was scared to think of Diana in with the bull."

"I was scared too."

He rubbed his thumb across the back of her hand and she couldn't breathe. "You were very brave going in after her the way you did."

"I had to get her out of there."

"I'll never forget what you did. Thank you."

"You're welcome."

"Am I forgiven, Laurel?"

She nodded. "Yes, I suppose so."

He laughed and squeezed her hand. "Don't take it so hard. What else can you do, but forgive me?"

She laughed. "Yes, what else?"

"You aren't one to hold a grudge."

"You're right." She tugged on her hand, but he held it tighter and lifted it to his lips and kissed it. Her heart beat so loud she was sure he could hear it over the crackle of the fire and the creaking of the house. Finally he released her hand and she stared at it, then up at him. "I don't understand you," she whispered.

"I don't understand myself." He raked his fingers through his hair.

She pushed back her chair and jumped up. "I'm

not hungry after all. I'm going to check on the children and go to bed."

In one fluid movement he stood before her and blocked her way. Their eyes locked and she couldn't move. He brushed a strand of hair off her cheek, leaving a trail of sparks. "Please forgive me for the way I've acted the past several weeks."

Her breast rose and fell. "Why have you been avoiding me, Morgan? I don't understand at all! What did I do?"

"Nothing, Laurel. It wasn't you, it was me. I found myself forgetting Rachel. That can't be."

"But you must forget her sometime!"

"No! It's not right. Not so soon!"

She saw the agony in his eyes and she couldn't argue with him. "I'd better check on Worth. He sometimes kicks his covers off and gets cold in the night." But she couldn't move away from Morgan. Outside a wolf howled. The lamp flickered, making the shadows on the wall jump.

"Try to understand, Laurel," Morgan said hoarsely.

She saw a muscle jump in his cheek. She wanted to slip her arms around him and have him hold her tight against him. Color stained her cheeks and she turned and walked away to check on the children.

CHAPTER 12

For Thanksgiving Morgan brought home a goose and Laurel roasted it and fixed a huge dinner that they all enjoyed. Snow covered the ground and Morgan took the children out to slide down a long hill north of the house. Laurel had begged to stay home and rest and relax. She'd been up since before dawn preparing the feast.

Gratefully she sat in the small rocker in front of the blazing fireplace and watched the flames leap up the stone chimney. This had been her home for almost eight months now and she couldn't imagine any other home for her, or any other family. It seemed as if a different person had lived with the Saunders and had taught school.

She closed her eyes and dozed, then awakened suddenly at a knock on the door. She ran to open it, expecting to see Morgan and the children too cold and snowy to turn the knob. Fred Saunders stood there, his hat in his hands and his nose and cheeks red with cold. His horse stood near the porch. "Fred!" she cried.

"May I come in?"

She glanced out at the snow covered yard for

Morgan and shivered as a blast of wind hit her. "I don't know. I'm alone."

"I must talk to you." He pushed past her into the warm kitchen and she slowly closed the door, shutting out the cold wind.

She looked at his gaunt face and the tired lines around his eyes. Was this the man she had loved? Her stomach tightened. "Morgan and the children will be back soon."

"This won't take long." He shrugged out of his heavy coat and held it over his arm. Red flannel underwear peeked out above the buttons and the cuffs of his thick plaid shirt. He studied Laurel thoughtfully. "Are you happy here?"

She shrugged and finally nodded. "Yes. Yes, I am. Very happy." Her pulse didn't quicken at his question or at the sight of him and knowing that pleased her and eased the guilt that seemed always at hand.

Fred smiled in relief. "I'm glad, Laurel."

"Is that why you came?"

"No." He cleared his throat. "We're moving."

Her eyes widened. "From Broken Arrow?"

"From Nebraska. I bought a place in Kansas and we're leaving tomorrow morning at the crack of dawn. It's only a day's ride away and the house is ready to move into."

"I am surprised that you're leaving, Fred." Laurel leaned back against the table and stared at him.

Fred shifted his coat to his other arm. "Laurel, I was a terrible husband to Jane."

She started to protest, but he held up his hand and

she closed her mouth.

"I was, and it wasn't because of you. I grew cold toward God and that left room in my life for Satan to do his dirty work. I lusted after you and that was wrong. Wrong to you and, even worse, a sin against my wife. I don't know how I could have let that happen!" He shook his head and blinked moisture from his eyes. "I want to make it up to Jane, but she remembers each time she sees you. I am going to take her away from here and we're going to start over."

Laurel trembled as shame washed over her.

"I love her. She stuck by me when she should have kicked me out in the cold. I don't deserve her." He rubbed a trembling hand over his face. "I had to tell you, Laurel, and I had to apologize for what I did to you. I want you to know that I've repented of my feelings toward you, and I mean to stay true to my wife from now on."

"I'm glad for that, Fred. Jane is a fine woman and she deserves the best." Laurel locked her hands behind her back and bit her bottom lip. "I am sorry that I ever let my feelings for you get out of hand. I was wrong!" She swallowed hard. "I was so afraid that your marriage would end because of me and I couldn't live with that."

"I know," whispered Fred.

She managed a shaky smile. "Have a wonderful life, Fred. And if ever you can tell Jane, tell her that I'm truly sorry and that I regard her highly."

Fred nodded. "I want you to have a good life, Laurel. Fill this home with love." He slipped on his coat. "Goodbye, Laurel. God bless you!"

"Goodbye, Fred." Laurel held the door open and watched as he walked to his horse and rode away. She shivered as a gust of wind blew snow against her. The sun sparkled off the snow. Slowly she closed the door and leaned against it.

Could she fill this house with love?

"Love," she whispered. "It's time to open my heart and see what's in it." She loved the children, but what were her feelings for Morgan?

She pushed the question aside, suddenly afraid of the answer.

She dropped a chunk of wood in the stove and made a pot of hot chocolate for her family. She slid it to the back of the stove to stay warm and walked to the front room. Carefully she laid a log in the fireplace and watched sparks fly up the chimney.

Laurel sank down on the small rocker and leaned her head back. This entire house was as familiar to her as the house she had lived in with Ma and Pa until they moved West. This was her home and it *was* up to her to fill it with love.

Could she learn to love Morgan Clements?

Her heart fluttered. Suddenly the kitchen door burst open and the children ran in, shouting for Ma to listen to their adventures in the snow. She walked to the kitchen and laughed as she looked at Morgan and the kids, all red-faced and covered with snow. She helped the children take off their wraps while they all talked at once. Morgan pulled off his coat and boots and stood by the stove warming his hands.

Laurel turned to him. "Did you have fun, Morgan?" The look on his face sent a shaft of fear through her. "What's wrong?"

"We'll talk about it later," he said.

She turned her attention from him back to the kids. She poured cups of cocoa for them and sat with them and listened as they talked. Morgan drank a cup of cocoa and talked only when it was necessary. Laurel knew their discussion would have to wait until the children were tucked in bed and asleep.

The rest of the afternoon seemed to drag. She played the piano and had the kids sing a song for Morgan that she'd taught them.

After they were asleep for the night, Laurel walked to the kitchen where Morgan sat at the table repairing Fly's bridle. She sank to her chair and locked her trembling hands in her lap. "Can we talk now?" she asked in a low, tense voice.

He laid aside the bridle and stood to his stocking feet. His shirt was unbuttoned, showing his gray longjohns and his shirt tail hung over his faded blue denims. The lamp cast a soft glow around the room. Wind whistled around the corner of the house. He stabbed his fingers though his dark hair and finally looked down at her. "I know Fred Saunders was here today."

She stood slowly and stepped away from the table and closer to Morgan. "He was."

"How could you ask him inside?"

"It was cold ouside!"

"Do you know how that made me feel?"

"Morgan, I can explain if you'll let me."

"I'm hurt and angry, Laurel! I don't know if I can

even listen."

"Can we sit down or do we stand here in the middle of the kitchen?"

"Sit if you want. I can't."

She took a deep, steadying breath. "Fred is moving."

Morgan slammed his fist to the table and the bridle jumped. "You can't go with him no matter how much you want to!"

She caught his fist with both her hands and held it. "Please, listen to me. Please, Morgan."

He slowly relaxed his fist and clasped her hand firmly, almost as if it was his lifeline. "Go ahead."

She saw the haunted look in his eyes and tears stung her eyes. "Fred and Jane are moving to Kansas." As quickly as she could, she told Morgan what Fred had said. "He is so sorry!"

"At least he was man enough to admit that he'd done wrong."

"Yes."

"That took courage."

She nodded.

"You're sure you're not upset?"

"Very sure."

"You honestly wouldn't have gone with him if he'd asked you?"

She laughed softly and squeezed his hand. "And give up all of this? This is my home now. I belong here."

With his free hand he stroked her soft cheek. "Yes, you sure do."

She leaned her face into his hand. "And so do

you."

"I do," he whispered.

She touched his face with her fingertips and he closed his eyes and groaned. She stepped closer to him. "Oh, Morgan," she whispered.

He released her hand and circled her waist with his strong arm pulling her close. She slid her arms around his neck and lifted her lips to his.

"Laurel," he said hoarsely. He lowered his head and touched his lips against hers. She returned his kiss with a hunger that surprised her. The kiss deepened and she wanted it to go on forever, but abruptly he pulled away, his face flushed. "I'm sorry, Laurel, That shouldn't have happened."

"Why not? I'm glad it did!" She slipped her arms around his neck again, but he pulled them down and stepped back.

"Don't! Do you think I can forget my wife so easily?"

She lifted her chin, flags of red flying in her cheeks and her dark eyes flashing. "*I* am your wife!"

He turned away, his head down. "Go to bed, Laurel. I'll close up and take care of things."

She stood motionless with tears burning her eyes, then turned and stumbled to her room. She crept onto the bed and curled up on top of the quilt, her eyes wide and a sob locked in her throat.

Several days later she held her hands out to the heat of the stove, shivering with cold as she forced back thoughts of Morgan's rejection. She looked over her shoulder at the children sitting on the floor putting on their boots. "Dress extra warm, kids. It's really cold out there." She'd just come in from hanging clothes on the line and her fingers still ached with cold. The clothes had whipped in the wind and froze as they whipped. Later she would carry them inside and hang them around the room to finish drying.

"Is it Christmas yet?" asked Diana as she reached for her heavy coat.

"Not yet," said Laurel, giving the same answer she had given since the week after Thanksgiving.

"When will it be?" asked Worth.

"Ten more days," said Hadley before Laurel could answer. "And we'll hang our stockings on the fireplace and Santa Claus will slide down the chimney and stuff our stockings full."

"He'll burn his bottom in the fire," said Worth. "He'll burn his bottom and he'll say, 'Ouch! I burned my bottom and I don't think I'll leave toys or candy for this family.' That's just what he'll say. Right, Ma?"

She laughed, thankful for a chance to laugh and forget the great sadness in her heart. Morgan didn't love her or want her as a true wife. He had made that very clear Thanksgiving night and he continued to make it clear by staying at a polite distance. He was always kind to her but he made sure he never touched her or got into a personal conversation with her. "We'll tell Pa to let the fire go out so that doesn't happen," she said, helping Worth slip on his mittens.

"I want a sled of my very own for Christmas,"

said Hadley. "And then we won't have to share one sled for all of us."

Laurel hid a smile. She knew Morgan was working on new sleds for all of them. She pictured how excited they'd be when they saw them Christmas morning. She was making a doll and doll clothes for Diana and mittens for all of them.

Hadley opened the door and cold air rushed in. Laurel walked to the door, watched the kids run out into the snow, then closed the door with a firm click. She lifted the cloth off the raised bread and smelled the yeasty dough. Quickly and expertly she formed the dough into loaves and put them in greased pans to rise. She peeled potatoes and set them in a pot of cold water off the stove, ready to slide them on the hot stove when it was time.

Just then the door banged open and she spun around to see Morgan, supporting Nick Stone. Both were covered with snow and looked and smelled cold. She ran to pull out a chair and Morgan eased Nick down on it.

"What happened?" she asked in alarm.

"I found him out by the lake, face down in the snow. I don't know how long he'd been there." Morgan eased off Nick's coat and Laurel toweled his hands and face dry.

"Nick," she said, peering into his red face. "Can you hear us?"

He barely nodded.

"We're going to take care of you. You're safe here with us." Laurel rubbed his salt and pepper hair dry while Morgan pulled off his boots and rubbed his feet.

"Why are you doing this?" asked Nick weakly.

"Doing what?" asked Morgan.

"Taking care of me."

Laurel frowned. "Did you think Morgan would let you freeze to death?"

"I would've done it to him," said Nick.

"Thankfully Morgan isn't like that," said Laurel crisply. "You should know what kind of man Morgan Clements is by now. He's good and kind." She turned to find Morgan watching her with hooded eyes. She tilted her chin and turned away. "I'll fix you a cup of coffee but, in the meantime, you hold your hands down in this pan of water so you don't lose your fingers to frostbite."

Morgan brought in a quilt and wrapped it around Nick and finally he stopped shivering. Morgan poured coffee for them and sat across from Nick. "I'm glad I found you now and not next spring. Did your horse throw you?"

"Yes. A rabbit spooked him and he shied. I had my mind on other things and I flew out of the saddle and landed hard on the ground. I tried to get up, but the wind was knocked right out of me. I don't think I was out there too long, but it seemed like forever."

Laurel set a plate of biscuits on the table with a jar of homemade tomato preserves. "You'll feel better after you drink your coffee and eat some of these."

Nick sipped the coffee, then spread a biscuit thick with butter and preserves. He cleared his throat.

"Are you going to ask me what I was doing on your property?" he asked gruffly.

"Should I?" asked Morgan as he leaned back and locked his hands behind his head.

"I would've shot first and asked questions later," said Nick.

"Times are changing, Nick," said Laurel. "This is no longer open range where you have to fight to keep what's yours. Properties are marked off clearly. We're not squatters, but we're legal land-owners."

"Laurel's right, Nick," said Morgan as he leaned forward. "You came to Nebraska while it was a territory and you had to fight to keep your grazing land and your water rights. You had an opportunity to buy the land with the lake on it, but you didn't. I did."

Nick threw up his hands. "I give up! I don't like it, but I reckon I have to go with the changing times. Or move to Dakota Territory!"

The men talked about changing times while Laurel churned butter. The children burst in and she helped them take off their wet, snowy things and sent them to their rooms to change into dry clothes. She fixed the fire and slid the loaves of bread into the hot oven to bake. The kids flocked back in, talking and laughing.

"Let's move to the front room away from this commotion," said Morgan as he helped Nick walk to the rockers to sit in front of the blazing fire-place.

Laurel poured glasses of milk for the kids and set

biscuits and butter out for them to eat. They told her about making angels in the snow and how fast they'd traveled on their sled.

"What's Nick Stone doing here?" whispered Diana.

"Your pa found him in the snow and brought him here."

Worth jumped up. "I want to sing to him and make him feel better."

Laurel caught Worth's arm and stopped him from running to the front room. "That's nice of you, but he and Pa are talking."

"They want to hear me sing," said Worth.

Since Worth had learned *Silent Night* he sang it to anyone who would listen. "You can sing for me later," said Laurel, kissing Worth's cheek. She checked the bread and when she turned around Worth was gone and she heard him singing in the front room. She rolled her eyes. Morgan would have to handle Worth.

Diana and Hadley ran to join Worth and Laurel laughed and shook her head. Nick Stone was in for a great time.

She pulled the bread from the oven and turned it out onto a cloth on the table, then smeared butter over the top. She fixed the fire and walked to the doorway just as Morgan and Nick joined in the singing. Nick had a very nice voice and he actually looked happy as he sang.

She glanced at Morgan in his rocker with Diana on his lap. They were both singing with gusto and didn't see Laurel. She watched Morgan's eyes twinkle and his dark brows lift. Love like a tiny flower budded inside her and blossomed. She dropped her hands to her sides and stood very still, her eyes wide in wonder. She loved Morgan Clements.

She loved him!

Could it be possible? As she watched him, the love grew and blossomed into something rare and beautiful that took her breath away.

She loved him with a passion that far surpassed the insipid feeling that she'd had for Fred Saunders. She backed away and leaned weakly against the kitchen wall, her hands at her sides and her eyes closed. She loved Morgan Clements!

What was she going to do now?

She had respected him, then grown to like him and now she loved him with an all-consuming love. Was this what Morgan felt for Rachel? No wonder he couldn't put Rachel aside and go on with life.

Tears welled up in Laurel's eyes and slipped down her flushed cheeks. She loved Morgan but he would never return that love. Could her love survive that? She moaned low in her throat and nodded. Her love would live forever.

Weakly she walked across the kitchen and looked out the window at the sun sparkling on the snow. She dabbed away her tears and sniffed. She loved Morgan Clements! And she would never be the same again.

"Is something wrong, Ma?" asked Hadley.

She turned and looked down at him and smiled. "Nothing's wrong, Hadley."

"Pa called you."

Her heart leaped. "He did?"

"He wants you to come play the piano for us. He sent me to get you when you didn't come when he called." Hadley tugged on her hand. "Will you come?"

Could she play the piano and sing without shouting out her love for Morgan? Was love shining from her in such glory that anyone looking at her would see?

"Ma?" Hadley tugged on her hand.

Finally she nodded. "I'll play for you for a while." She gripped his hand and walked to the front room with him. Her eyes met Morgan's and, for a split second, the world stood still. It seemed as if they were totally alone in the entire world. Hadley tugged on her hand and she turned to the piano, her cheeks flaming.

"What should I play?" She looked down at her long fingers on the ivory keys, willing her heart to stop leaping.

Everyone called out a different song, but Worth's voice rang out over the others. She ran her fingers over the keys and sang out clearly and boldly with the others. Soon everyone stood around her. Morgan rested his hands lightly on her shoulders and every part of her body felt his touch.

Later they sat at the dinner table, eating and talking. She noticed that Nick Stone looked like a different man.

"This has been one of the happiest days of my life," he said as he looked around the table. "Thank you all very much."

"Come again soon," said Morgan. "And bring your sister."

"I will. I think she would like to come."

"Come for Christmas if you want," said Laurel.

"We're going to put out the fire in the fireplace so Santa Claus won't burn his bottom," said Worth.

Everyone laughed and Worth looked puzzled. "It's not funny," he said, his face red. "Santa Claus is my friend and I don't want him to get burned."

Morgan ruffled Worth's hair. "That's right. We don't hurt our friends, do we?"

Nick cleared his throat. "Nor your enemies." He pushed back his chair and stood behind it. "I want to thank all of you for this day. Morgan, I promise that I won't do anything more to try to get the lake or your homestead from you. I was wrong."

"Is he our friend now, Pa?" asked Diana.

"I am if you'll have me," said Nick.

"We'll have you," said Morgan as he walked to Nick with his hand out. The men clasped hands and the children cheered.

Nick turned to Laurel with his hand out and she clasped it warmly. "Morgan's a lucky man to have you, Laurel."

"Thank you." She wanted to peek at Morgan, but she didn't dare. Did he consider himself lucky to have her?

Nick stepped back. "I'm ready when you are, Morgan. Are you sure you can spare the time to drive me home?"

Morgan nodded. "I can make it home in time for

chores." He grabbed his heavy coat and handed Nick's to him. "We'll use the sleigh and cut across the prairie." He turned to Laurel. "Be back before dark."

"Be careful." She stood at the window and watched them walk to the barn. Love for Morgan flowed out from her to him and when she saw him turn and look toward the house she wondered if he could feel it. He lifted his hand in a wave and she waved back. "I love you," she mouthed.

CHAPTER 13

Her heart racing with thoughts of love for Morgan, Laurel paced the kitchen while the children slept. By the time they were up from their naps, Morgan would probably be home. Time seemed to stand still. She sighed. "I'll work on the Christmas gifts," she said. "It'll make the time go faster." She wrinkled her nose. "And maybe take my mind off Morgan."

She walked to her bedroom where she had hidden the gifts in her trunk. She knelt down to open the bottom dresser drawer where she stored the extra fabric. She would make a little calico dress for Diana's doll. She pulled out the material and pushed the drawer shut. It caught on something just as it did each time she tried to close it, but this time she couldn't force it shut. With a frown she tugged it out until the drawer rested on the floor. Laurel peeked inside the dresser and found a small black book at the very back, some of the pages open and crumpled. She pulled the book out. "A diary," she muttered. She opened the front cover. A tingle ran through her as she saw that it was Rachel's diary. Her mouth turned cotton dry and she couldn't move for a minute. Finally she laid the diary aside and pushed the drawer back in place.

She walked to the front room with the diary clutched in her hand. Butterflies fluttered in her stomach. Dare she read Rachel's private words?

She sank to the rocker and opened it to the first page. She had to know what Rachel had written. She wanted to know what Rachel had thought and felt as she lived and loved here in this home. Taking a deep breath, Laurel started reading.

I have finally found the time to start a diary. I hope it's not too late. I know deep in my heart that I'm not going to live long and I want to put down my feelings and my thoughts to help me through the days ahead. I know God has an answer for me, but I can't seem to find it. I know that Jesus is my healer, but I don't have the faith to believe.

Laurel groaned and read on as the fire crackled and burned brightly and Rachel's children slept soundly in the other room.

I look at my beautiful children and my wonderful husband and I wonder how I can leave them. Many times I wake up in the night and sob into my pillow so that Morgan can't hear me. I don't want him to know that I'm a coward or that I'm going to die.

Today I decided that I should tell Morgan that I'm going to die. Oh, my, but it's hard to do! He will be crushed. We've been together nine years and he doesn't take change easily. I know he'll miss me and I know that he loves me, but his love was never the grand passion that mine was for him. It's hard for me to imagine life without my darling Morgan, even life in heaven where I'll be whole and healthy and happy with Jesus. How I wish I knew how to receive my healing here on earth! I've searched the Scriptures and I know healing is mine, but I'm so tired that I can't grasp the faith to stand firm on God's Word until I'm well again. And Morgan doesn't know how to help me. He loves the Lord and he's strong in many areas, but not where healing is concerned. My darling Morgan!

Laurel wiped away a tear and closed her eyes for a moment before she continued to read.

We were both so young when we decided to get married. I loved him and I would've gone anywhere with him. I was thankful to get away from my family. They are very worldly and they think I am a fanatic. They don't like my faith in God or my high standards. But Morgan has the same love for God and the same standards.

We were so proud when Hadley was born! And then beautiful Diana came along and our precious Worth. Poor little Worth has a sickness that flares up every once in a while. The doctor doesn't know what causes it, but he said it is important that Worth get plenty of rest, good food and fresh air. And when the fever does come, bring it down as quickly as possible.

Now I'm carrying our fourth baby. Something must be wrong for I am always tired. So tired! The doctor can't do anything for me. Both the baby and I are going to die. The precious baby won't have a chance to know his brothers or sister or father.

With a moan Laurel closed the diary and leaned back again. The fire snapped. Wind howled around the corner of the house. She rubbed the cover of the diary. Should she read Rachel's private thoughts? "I'll put it away for the children when they grow up," she whispered. But she opened the diary and flipped through the pages until her own name leaped out at her. Laurel gasped and gripped the book tighter as she read.

Morgan can't raise the family alone, nor can he be alone. I have considered the women that I know and that I've met and I believe that Laurel Bennett would be a good mother for my children and a loving wife for my Morgan.

I've talked to Laurel only a few times, but I've watched her life and I know she is a good woman. She is not selfish like Rebecca. My sister would force herself on Morgan if she could because she thinks he's handsome and she knows he's not dirt poor like so many homesteaders. And in Morgan's grief he might turn to Rebecca because she is my sister and because he knows the children need a mother. I can't allow this to happen. I talked to him about Laurel Bennett and he was too angry to listen. But I will convince him for his own good. He doesn't want me to die and, God help me, I don't want to die! I just want to feel better! I know Laurel would make my home a good home. She is intelligent and has more schooling than I have. She and Morgan would have much in common. He likes to read and study and I was never good at either. She is brave and strong and made of real pioneer stock.

*Little by little I will persuade Morgan to marry
her. I will make him promise or I know he will not
survive on his own with the children. He is fine and
strong but, in his grief, the wrong woman could
pull him down and destroy his dream for this place
and our children.*

*I have tried to convince Morgan to open his heart
to love again, but he is so stubborn that he won't
listen to me. He says that he has given in and will
marry Laurel Bennett, but that he will feel guilty
if he gives her his heart.*

Laurel bit back a sob. "Rachel knew Morgan so
well! He could care for me, I think." She brushed a
tear away and read on.

*Love must be nurtured, tended like a garden or it
will die. He can't continue to love me the way he
does now because I won't be here to nurture that
love. I've told him that but he won't listen. Secretly it pleases me to think that he will love me
always and not love another, but that's bad of me to
feel that way. He must love again and maybe this
time he will love with the burning passion that I
have felt for him.*

*I would like to talk to Laurel Bennett before I die
and tell her my thoughts, but Morgan made me
promise not to. I have kept my promise. If I could
speak to her I would tell her to love Morgan well.
I would tell her to break down the barriers that he
is sure to build so that his heart is free to love again.
I would tell her never to give up. Love will blossom!*

God, bless my family and may love grow until it

surrounds them all!

Laurel pressed the book to her heart as tears flowed down her cheeks. She would put the diary away again, but she would take it out another time to read all the pages. Then she would save it to show Morgan and the children someday how very much Rachel loved them.

Laurel tucked the diary away in her dresser just as the children woke from their naps and called to her. She brushed away her tears, blew her nose and said, "I'm coming, kids."

A few minutes later she stoked the fire in the cookstove, then suddenly realized how late it was. The children had slept later than usual and it was already growing dark and was time to do the chores. She frowned as she grabbed the milk pail. Where was Morgan?

She opened the door and gasped as she saw snow swirl across the porch.

"Snow!" cried Worth, jumping around beside her.

"A blizzard," said Hadley with a shiver.

"Where's Pa?" asked Diana in a tiny voice. They all knew of people who had gotten lost and died in blizzards.

"He'll be back," said Laurel, keeping her voice light. "God is with him and he has angels protecting him."

"I hope the angels have on warm coats," said Worth.

Laurel pulled on Morgan's old coat, wrapped her scarf around her head and neck and slipped on her boots. "Stay inside, kids. It's blowing and snowing too hard for you to take care of the chickens tonight. I'll do it myself." She trembled as she looked out again. Could she even find the chicken coop and the barn? Last winter Granville Packard had walked right past his barn and out into the open prairie. They found him a few weeks later frozen stiff a few feet from the barn. She forced back a shiver as she turned to the kids. "Stay inside and talk about Christmas. Hadley, fix the fire the way I taught you. And no matter how long it takes me outside, don't come after me! You hear me, Worth?"

He nodded.

"I'll be back." She walked onto the porch and snow stung her face and swirled around her body. She could barely see the chicken coop. She ducked her head and walked to the pump for water. She fed and watered the chickens and gathered the few eggs. They had been laying poorly since the cold snap hit.

She bent into the wind and trudged toward the barn. Snow clung to her lashes and the pieces of hair that had escaped her scarf. Wind whipped snow around her, almost blinding her. Where was the barn? Bessie would already be waiting in her stall. Laurel stopped, her heart beating hard. Had she missed the barn? Would she walk right out into the prairie like Granville had?

She peered through the snow and finally identified the big black shape of the barn. She missed the door, but inched along the barn until she found it. She walked inside, glad to be out of the angry blizzard. Her hands were numb as she lit the lantern and hung it back on its peg. Kitty rubbed her leg and mewed. "I know it's cold, Kitty. Aren't you glad you have this nice barn to live in?"

Laurel threw hay to Fly and the bull that Morgan had put in the corral next to the barn a few days ago.

"Morgan, where are you? Protect him, Lord. Bring him home safely. Thank you, Father."

Maybe he would stay at Nick's until the blizzard stopped. But what if that was days from now? She bit her lip and groaned.

She fed Bessie and perched on the milkstool, squirting warm, foamy milk into the bucket. After filling Kitty's bowl with milk, she turned out the lantern and headed out into the blizzard for the terrible trek to the house. Wind whistled around her and tore at her skirts. Snow almost blinded her but a tiny light from the house led her in the right direction.

Inside the house she stamped snow from her boots and it skittered across the floor where the children touched it and laughed. She shivered and wondered if she'd ever be warm again.

"Is Pa back?" asked Hadley as he peered out the window with his hands cupped around his face and his nose pressed against the cold pane.

"Not yet," said Laurel. "But he'll come home."

She fed them supper and later popped corn for them to eat while she read aloud in the flickering light of the lamp. The evening seemed to stretch on and on. After tucking the children into bed, she paced the floor praying for Morgan. Finally she sat at the piano and played song after song after song until her fingers ached.

Suddenly the kitchen door banged open, then shut and she jumped up and ran to see Morgan just inside the door, covered with snow and looking more like a snowman than a real person.

"The chores?" he whispered through chattering teeth.

"I took care of them," she said as she pushed him down on a chair and tugged off his icy gloves and hat and scarf. He shook so hard she could barely peel off his coat. His face was frosted and she carefully wiped it off. She ran for a quilt and made him undress by the kitchen stove and wrap in the quilt. "Come sit in your rocker." She tugged on his arm and helped him to the rocker in front of the blazing fire. He fell back in his chair and held the quilt tightly around him as he shivered. Laurel stuck a log in the fire and sparks shot up the chimney. Outdoors the wind howled and rattled the windows. Worth cried out in his sleep and Laurel went to pull his covers back over him. She grabbed another quilt from her bed and laid it over Morgan.

"I missed the house," he said, his voice unsteady. "And then I heard the piano and I headed for the sound. If you had stopped playing, I wouldn't have found the house."

"Oh, Morgan!" She sank back in her rocker and stared at him. " I was so frightened for you!"

"I should have stayed at Nick's, but I couldn't stand to think of you and the kids here alone during such a terrible blizzard. Who knows how long it might last?"

"I know." Often she had seen blizzards last from one day to a week. "I'm thankful you're home."

I think I can get dressed now and I'd sure like something to eat. I smell popcorn, don't I?" He grinned and she wanted to fling herself into his arms.

"The kids ate it all. But I'll make you more." She gave him clean long underwear, socks, blue denims and a warm shirt. "I'll go heat up stew for you."

A few minutes later she set the bowl of stew on the table just as he walked in looking as if nothing had happened to him. She looked up at him and burst into tears.

"Laurel! What's wrong?"

"You're home," she said.

"I know." He lifted her apron tail and wiped away her tears. "And I'm safe. So are you and the kids. Sit down with me, will you?"

She nodded and sniffed back a sob. "This was a long, long day."

"Yes, yes it was." He rubbed a lean finger along her cheek, leaving a flaming trail where he touched her. He smiled and the smile zoomed to her heart. "I'd better eat. I'm beginning to feel a little light-headed."

She was feeling a lot light-headed, but she didn't say so. She sat beside him and drank a glass of water while he ate three bowls of stew and almost a whole loaf of bread. She loved watching him, the shape of his hand, the intent look on his face as he ate, the twinkle in his eye when he said something to her. She smiled. "I'm looking forward to Christmas, aren't you, Morgan?"

He nodded.

"We'll find a tree as soon as the blizzard is over and put it up in the front room in front of the south window and we'll decorate it," she said.

"We have some decorations around here somewhere that Rachel made." A haunted look crossed his face, then was gone.

Laurel touched his hand and he looked at her. "I am here for you, Morgan. I am here to take away your loneliness and to help you with Christmas and all the other days. Rachel is happy and at peace in heaven. We are here. Together. We'll add to the Christmas decorations that Rachel made and we'll keep hers so that we never forget that she was once a part of this family."

Tears glistened in his dark eyes and he quickly blinked them away. "She made this house a home."

"I know, and now I'll do that. But not just me, you and the kids and me together."

He nodded. "That is what Rachel wanted for us."

"Yes. It is."

"I wonder."

"What?" she whispered.

"I don't have to feel guilty that it's happened. That together you and I have made this a home." He sounded as if he was talking to himself, sorting out his own feelings and Laurel sat quietly beside him, letting him work through it. "We are a family here, you and me and the kids. Nick pointed it out to me today. He was very envious."

"He needs a wife. I wonder if I could get him and Ganny Blake together."

Morgan threw back his head and laughed a great shout of a laugh. "That would be worth seeing, wouldn't it?" Morgan jumped up and spread his arms wide. "I can see it now. Ganny and Nick united in holy matrimony. Who would swing the first blow?"

Laurel laughed as she stacked the dishes in the dishpan and wiped off the table. "I don't know if it would come to that, Morgan. I know they both have very strong personalities, but love can conquer all. If they fell in love, they'd live happily ever after." She stood before Morgan and looked up into his dark eyes. "Love is a powerful force."

"You should know. You and Fred Saunders."

She lifted her chin a fraction and stood with her hands at her waist. "I never knew the force of love before. That little feeling I had for Fred Saunders was more like a schoolgirl's crush. What's in my heart now is a raging fire that blazes stronger each moment."

He grew very quiet. A muscle jumped in his firm jaw. "Anyone I know?"

She laughed lightly, stepped forward, reached up and kissed him full on the lips. "Good night, Morgan. Sweet dreams."

She walked to her room, stopped in the middle of it and tried to calm the wild beat of her heart over her daring actions. Finally she was able to undress, slip on her long flannel nightgown, braid her hair, pray and climb into bed.

The next morning Morgan was already in the kitchen when Laurel walked in to start the fire. One already blazed in the cookstove and the teakettle boiled merrily. "Good morning," she said with a bright smile. Could he hear the wild beat of her heart?

"Good morning," he said, smiling. "I'm just on my way to milk Bessie."

She glanced out the window to see the ground piled with snow, but the sky bright. "I'm glad the blizzard stopped. You'll have a time walking to the barn, though."

"The drifts are packed hard enough to hold my weight." He pulled on his heavy coat and clamped his hat on. He reached for the door and she stopped him.

"Wrap this around your neck." She slipped a wool scarf around his neck and tucked it in the top of his coat. "And take this to keep you warm." She kissed first one cheek and then the other. He needed to shave, but she liked the feel of his whiskers.

"Laurel! What's gotten into you?" he asked, blushing.

She laughed up at him. "I'm happy. Aren't you?"

He shrugged. "Maybe. I reckon so."

"Then let it show, Morgan!" She caught his hands and danced him around the room, laughing at the look on his face.

He pulled free with a chuckle. "You're a crazy woman this morning. I think it's the Christmas fever, or something."

"Or something," she said softly.

He scooped up the milk pail and walked out into the snow. She wanted to shout after him that she loved him wildly, passionately, but she closed the door to shut out the cold and started breakfast.

As the day wore on the temperature rose and by afternoon it was warm enough to bundle the children up for outdoors. "We'll all build a snowman together," Laurel said, grinning.

Outdoors she found a clear spot near the end of the porch and showed the kids how to roll the snow to make a snowman. Laurel's dark eyes sparkled and her cheeks grew rosy red.

Suddenly a snowball splattered against her back. She spun around. The kids fell into the snow, giggling. "Who did that?" she shouted, pretending to be angry. "Who dared to hit me with a snowball?"

"Not me!" cried Worth, tumbling through the snow until he looked like a snowman with bright blue eyes.

"Not me!" Diana and Hadley shouted together as they laughed.

Laurel marched out onto the snowbank and shielded her eyes against the sun and snow. "Who hit me with a snowball?" she shouted at the top of her lungs.

Another snowball struck her arm.

"It's Pa!" shouted the children as they danced around and laughed.

"Where is he?" Laurel turned slowly, looking all around. "Where are you, Morgan Clements?" She spotted him at the corner of the house. Bending over and scooping up a handful of snow, she made it into a firm, round ball and threw it. It hit the house, leaving a circle of snow. Morgan peeked out and she threw another one, just missing his head but letting snow fall into his collar.

"This is war!" he shouted. He aimed snowball after snowball at her, hitting almost every time.

She ran toward him, laughing until she could barely breathe as she pitched snowballs at him, missing every time. She glanced over her shoulder at the children. "Kids, let's get Pa!"

With loud whoops they ran at him, hurling snowballs.

Suddenly Laurel fell back in the snow. "I give up! I'm too tired to throw another snowball!"

Morgan knelt beside her with a laugh. His face was red and wet and he'd lost his hat. "What happened here? Did you lose the fight?"

"I guess I did." She suddenly felt like a little girl again.

The children tumbled down the snowbank and ran to work on the snowman again, their voices ringing happily through the air. A horse neighed. From inside the chicken coop, a rooster crowed.

Morgan held a handful of snow over Laurel. "Would you say I won the fight?" He grinned as he moved the handful of snow closer and closer to her face. "Did I win, or not?"

She lunged up at him, taking him by surprise and knocked him backward in the snow. She fell on him, laughing into his face as she reached for some snow.

"Oh, no you don't!" He flipped her off him and pinned her under him. "You have had it now, Laurel Clements!" He rubbed a handful of snow in her face as she thrashed around, laughing and screaming for him to stop. "Do you give?" he asked, laughing.

"I give! I give!"

He rubbed the snow off her face and sat her up in front of him as he hunkered down before her.

She leaned forward, almost touching her face to his. "I love you," she whispered.

He dropped back from her, startled. "Why did you say that?" he asked gruffly.

"Because it's true." She smiled and tenderly touched his red cheek. "I love you, Morgan. I love you!"

"Don't, Laurel. Please don't say that."

She flung her arms around him, sending him backward in the snow again and kissed him hard on the lips, then leaped up and ran from him, laughing gaily. She stopped on the porch and looked at him where he stood on the snowbank. She cupped her snowy mittens around her mouth and shouted, "I love you, Morgan Clements!"

The children turned from the snowman and shouted, "I love you, Pa!" They thought it was a new game and they shouted it over and over, laughing hard.

Morgan spun around and stalked over the packed snowbanks to the barn.

Laurel chuckled and walked to the door. "Kids, time to come in. We'll finish the snowman later."

She waited for Morgan to come in so she could see

him and talk to him. Butterflies fluttered in her stomach as she wondered what he would say to her. What would she do if he totally rejected her? She shook her head. She wouldn't let that happen.

At suppertime he finally walked in. He ate in silence. Several times she felt him watching her, but each time she looked at him, he lowered his eyes. She tried to keep up her usual table talk but ran out of things to say, so she listened to the children and left Morgan alone.

Later she put the children to bed, almost too tired to read and pray with them. Tonight she would be glad to fall into bed and sleep. All the exercise of playing in the snow and the stress with Morgan was taking its toll.

She walked to the front room to find Morgan in his rocker, his feet stretched toward the fire and a book in his hand. He looked up from the book and her pulse quickened.

"Good night," she said softly.

He cleared his throat. "Did you mean what you said outside?"

Her heart skipped a beat, then thudded so loud she was sure he could hear it over the snap of the fire. "What did I say?"

He stood and the book fell to the floor. "That you love me."

She nodded, watching for a sign from him. "I meant it."

"I don't know what to say."

"You don't have to say anything. I just wanted you to know how I feel. It just sort of spilled out."

She shrugged.

"It made me feel...strange."

She cocked her head. "It shouldn't. I am your wife. You are my husband. It's all right to love each other."

He walked to her and touched her face with the very tips of his fingers. "You're right. It is."

"It really is," she whispered, hardly daring to breathe.

He slipped his strong arms around her and slowly and gently pulled her to him. He bent his head, hesitated, then kissed her. He pulled away and she wanted to kiss him again, but she waited for him. He looked into her wide brown eyes, the soft curve of her cheeks and her full pink lips. A flame sparked in his eyes and she almost melted in his arms. "Laurel?" he whispered.

"I love you," she mouthed.

"I love you," he said hoarsely.

Her heart leaped. "You do?"

He nodded. "I tried not to."

"Because of Rachel?"

"Yes." He sighed. "But I couldn't make the love for you stop growing. One day it was a tiny spark and then it filled me so full that I couldn't think of anyone or anything but you."

"Oh, Morgan," she whispered. His words left her weak with a longing that she'd never felt before. She pushed her fingers into the dark thickness of the hair on the back of his head. "I love you," she said softly.

He kissed her again as if he would never quit,

then he buried his face in her hair and groaned, "Laurel, Laurel. What's happening to me?"

"You tell me," she said with her mouth close to the firm brown column of his neck.

"It's love," he whispered. "Love like I've never felt before. Is it wrong for me to feel this way so soon after Rachel?"

Laurel moved and cupped his face in her hands, looking deep into his eyes. "It's not wrong. How can love between a husband and wife be wrong?"

He scooped her up in his strong arms and sat in his rocker with her cradled in his lap. A log settled in the fireplace. A wolf howled in the distance. "Let's talk about what's happening here," he said.

She nuzzled his cheek. "Let's talk about love." She looked at him with a teasing sparkle in her eyes.

"Sometimes it doesn't take words," he said. He tightened his arms around her and kissed her to let her know talking was over for now. She snuggled deeper into his arms and gave herself up to his kisses.